I0587518

DUST AND KISSES

A SEEDERS UNIVERSE PREQUEL NOVEL

DEAN WESLEY SMITH

wmg
PUBLISHING

Dust and Kisses
Copyright © 2020 by Dean Wesley Smith
First published in Smith's Monthly #1, WMG Publishing, October,
2013
Published by WMG Publishing
Cover and Layout copyright © 2020 by WMG Publishing
Cover design by Allyson Longueira/WMG Publishing
Cover art copyright © kwest / Depositphotos

ISBN: 13 - 978-1-56146-247-6
ISBN: 10 - 1-56146-247-0

ALSO BY DEAN WESLEY SMITH

For Kris, always the love of my life,

And Janis Ian and Mike Resnick,
two great writers who sparked this novel.
Thanks.

PROLOGUE

IF SHE HAD THOUGHT ABOUT IT, Carey Noack would have figured that the world would end in a big build-up, with lots of panic and time to say good-bye to loved-ones in tragic scenes of crying and hugging like it always was in the movies. But she had never thought about it. None of her friends read science fiction, and the closest thing she had come to an end of the world thought was worrying about how the Greenland ice cap might melt.

So Wednesday morning, when the world did end, she wasn't expecting it. No one was, actually. But she did remember the exact moment it happened, right down to the second because her job that morning was to stare at scientific measuring instruments and a clock while taking notes about the readings every fifteen seconds.

At 23, she had gotten lucky in life, and she figured in love as well. A post-doc in astrophysics from the University of Oregon, she had landed a plum job working in Portland, Oregon for the famous Dr. Canfield, a man she both admired and hated, often in the same breath when talking to her friends and family. She stood at five-foot-two, a good sixteen inches shorter than Canfield who looked like a cross between a bad Dicken's character and a stretched Santa Claus because of his white beard. She had long, brown hair and brown eyes that everyone said were "fiery" whatever that meant.

Canfield had gotten the habit of patting her on the head like a child every time he was pleased with her, and if she didn't need the job working with him so much for her career, she would have just broken his hand in about a dozen places. If he caught her on the wrong day, she still might. Screw the career.

Her fiancée, Paine Kennedy, worked as an assistant coach at the University, and even though with her working for Canfield in Portland, the two-hour drive down I-5 between the cities didn't stop them from having a wonderful relationship, one they both planned on turning into a marriage next year. This morning, she had kissed him good-bye at seven while he tried to grope her to get her to come back to bed. As much as she wanted to rejoin the man of her dreams in that bed, she didn't dare be late for work. So she had left him to go back to sleep with a promise she would see him at lunch.

Lunch didn't happen. At 10:18 and seven seconds on Wednesday morning, the world ended.

At 10:18, she was sitting in a protected steel vault watching the "control" readings for an experiment Canfield was doing in another room. Canfield's hope was to get some variance between two readings, hers in a protected control vault and his in the open.

At 10:22, as planned, she logged in her last readings and the exact time and opened the vault door.

Dr. Canfield lay sprawled on the floor of the lab, his eyes rolled up into his head.

For an instant, the sight shocked her. Then she quickly moved, grabbing the phone on the desk above Canfield and jabbing in 911.

"Don't you die on me now!" she said to the thin man.

While it rang, she tucked the phone under her chin and knelt beside him, feeling for a pulse.

Nothing that she could find.

She quickly flipped him onto his back and went through the quick procedures she had learned in her first aid class three years before. With the phone still ringing in her ear, she started pumping on his chest.

"Come on, damn-it! Answer!"

She kept at it, working to keep her pace steady, her pressure solid on his chest, but not too hard.

No answer. The phone just kept ringing.

After about a minute, she knew she couldn't wait any longer. She needed help, and no one was coming into the lab to give her help. She needed to go find help if Canfield had a chance of pulling through this.

Leaving the phone connected to 911 and ringing, she checked for a pulse on Canfield, then ran for the door, heading down the lab hallway and out onto the street to get help from someone.

She burst through the exterior door and took two staggering steps before stopping on the hot sidewalk between two tall buildings.

The sound hit her first.

At least a hundred car alarms in the surrounding blocks of the city were going off at once.

She looked around, trying to grasp what she was seeing.

The morning promised a hot day ahead. Two blocks down the hill was the Willamette River, two blocks to her left was Burnside, a major arterial through the city. The buildings around here were ten to thirty stories tall. Canfield's lab was on the main floor, tucked to the back of the building.

An intersection with a streetlight was to her right about fifty paces, and parked cars lined the street.

Everything was so familiar. She had seen it all every day for months.

Then her mind suddenly let her see what was wrong.

Nothing was moving.

Bodies lay crumpled in piles along the sidewalk going in both directions from her. Cars had crashed into other cars, their drivers slumped against their seat belts, heads rolled to one side or the other.

She ran to the nearest woman on the sidewalk and checked her.

Dead.

She checked another woman.

And then another.

All dead.

She could see hundreds of bodies around her, all seemingly dead.

Bio attack? Terrorist attack? What had happened?

"Help, someone!" she shouted, but her voice was drowned by the massive wave of noise from the car alarms and running engines.

No one was alive to hear her.

Then the smiling image of her fiancée flashed into her mind and she screamed "Paine!"

He was fifteen blocks away.

She turned and headed for her apartment in the northwest section of town at a run, jumping over bodies, trying not to look at them, trying to ignore the dead staring at her from their still running cars.

The nightmare had begun. The world had ended.

She was still alive.

And very much alone.

ONE

THREE YEARS from the day the world ended, Carey Noack stood on the abandoned freeway overpass and wondered exactly where she was going to stay that night.

In front of her, the gray of the dead city of Portland, Oregon, filled the hillside for miles in all directions. Beside her, the deep blue of the gently flowing Willamette River moved silently past. She figured she had every building in the city to pick from. Apartments, houses, hotel suites, and those really nice condos she remembered being down on the river. For all anyone would care, she could set up camp right in the middle of the old city hall. She doubted anyone was left alive there. From what she had understood of the old city politics, there hadn't been much life there before everyone died.

Actually, there were two places she wasn't going to stay. Her old apartment and her parents home out in Beaverton. Both those places weren't options because the bodies of Paine and her mother were still there. But just about every other building was, unless she actually found someone else alive and living here.

She hoped for that. Dreamed about that.

Didn't expect it.

It had been exactly three years ago to the day that the city and almost everyone in it, and in the world, had died, sending her running eventually to the Oregon coast to get away from the smell of a million dead.

Now, on today of all days, like celebrating some sick birthday, she was back, facing the city again. Facing the nightmares of having everyone die around her.

"Such a brave little girl," she said aloud, then shook her head. As a child, her mother said that to her all the time, every time Carey started to feel sorry for herself. Over the last three years, she had repeated that saying a lot to keep from going completely crazy.

Carey leaned her backpack and rifle against the edge of the overpass, then levered her short frame up onto the concrete guardrail so she could get a better view of what was ahead.

It was a good fifty feet to the surface of the freeway below her. The warm wind coming from the direction of the Columbia River Gorge jostled her, so she spread her feet for a better stance. She worked and exercised so much; she didn't have an extra ounce of fat on her body, and often felt a good wind could turn her into the Flying Nun without even having to wear a stupid-looking hat.

Her light-brown hair, left long and pulled back out of the way, whipped at the side of her head and shoulders. She had let her hair grow long mostly because she didn't feel like she had the skill to do anything else with it. Besides, who else was going to see it?

She glanced down at her arm to make sure she wasn't burning in the hot sun. Her skin was light, with freckles, and she had smothered it every day on this trip with lotion. At times, she had so much lotion on, she felt that if she fell down, she would slide like a kid on one of those old Slip-and-Slides her dad bought for the back yard. He'd only tried it once and instead of sliding, did a belly-flop, cracked a rib, and hadn't bothered to try again. Carey remembered her mother hadn't stopped laughing for days.

She slid her hand along her arm. She was greased up like a Thanksgiving bird, enough so that at the moment there was no sign of burning. Good.

She stood there on the overpass, hands on hips like Superwoman, staring into the dead city. For her grand entrance back, she had worn a black sleeveless tee-shirt, jeans, and her favorite tennis shoes. As she was looking into a mirror this morning, the old worry of being underdressed in the big city came flooding back. It was amazing how old habits died hard.

She glanced down at the wreck-strewn freeway below the overpass. "Man, Carey, how stupid is this trip?"

Her words echoed against the pavement and vanished into the silence of the warm wind.

Stupid. She knew the answer.

Shaking her head, she jumped back off the railing and grabbed a small towel from her pack to wipe the sweat from her face and arms. The weather had turned out to be one of those typical Oregon late-summer days, where the bright sun and clear skies made the air feel hotter than it actually was. And on top of that, the wind from the Gorge was sweeping in even warmer air from the state's central deserts, heating up the valley and the city of Portland like an oven.

She couldn't say, standing there in the center of the freeway overpass, that she had missed that dry, brittle wind during her years away. It seldom got above seventy degrees where she lived overlooking the beach and the waves of the Pacific Ocean. She loved the coolness, the constant pounding of the surf, the fresh, crisp air. But she had also loved this city three years ago.

And right now, if forced, she would admit she still missed it.

She finished wiping off her arms, put the towel back in her pack, and grabbed the water bottle. She was going to have to be careful, make sure she didn't push too hard. The last thing she would need would be to get heat stroke.

She leaned against the concrete side of the overpass and let her mind drift back three years. She didn't remember much about those nightmarish last days she had spent in the city, and the trip escaping to the coast. The overriding memory was of the bodies everywhere, the smell of death growing by the moment, and her desire to run as far away as possible.

The house she had found on the coast was just north of a little town called Depoe Bay. The house sat on a rock ledge jutting out into the ocean, and sprawled over three floors, with windows on all levels facing the empty sea. The breezes were always off the water, and seldom did the smell of death reach her.

Nothing to see, nothing to smell, nothing to remind her that almost all of the human race had suddenly died.

Also, the house was hidden from view of anyone who *might* be left alive, and who *might* be moving along the coastal highway. That distance from the road gave her a sense of safety. She knew there had to be others who survived besides her. She didn't know how many, or where they were. But if she had survived, others had as well.

Her biggest, "ugly fear," as her mother would call it, was what someone else would do if they found her. The safest way to get around that fear was to not push the question. Her old, and now dead friends had called her "plucky." But being plucky didn't defend her from someone who wanted to rape or kill her. Being smart did, and the house allowed her lots of smart options.

So, she had a nice, safe, *smart* place there to live. Why, after three long years of living alone, safe, on the coast, was she back in the dead city risking her life?

Was she really that lonely?

Did she really think that there might be a group of survivors living here?

Maybe. Maybe not.

She should just turn around and go back to her cats.

Damn, she missed her cats.

She hoped she had left enough food for them to make it until she got back. Since she had nothing else to worry about beside herself, she tended to be over-protective of her two cats. Centaur was a yellow tabby with one bad eye, and Princess a small female with pure white fur. She really missed them. Maybe she should head back and forget this stupid exploring.

"Such a brave little girl," she said out loud, staring at the dead city. "You've come this far, see this through."

She studied some of the details around her. Windows in nearby buildings were covered with dirt and film, weeds were growing thick in the cracks of the sidewalks, and nothing was lit. She had seen parts of the city look like that when it still had hundreds of thousands of people in it.

No power to be seen, and she hadn't expected any. The power on the coast had gone down the first winter, and nowhere along the way from the coast had she seen any place with power. The stoplights at the end of the overpass were now nothing more than dead eyes hanging over deserted streets. It gave her a sudden feeling that someone was watching her.

Could that be possible?

She studied the area around her, turning slowly. Nothing moved besides the leaves on the trees and the weeds blowing in the wind.

She did a second slow circle, staring at the blank windows, the dead cars scattered everywhere, the over-grown weeds.

Nothing.

No one was watching her. There weren't that many people left alive who could.

She shook off the feeling, took a second, long drink from the bottle of water, and stood on the overpass, just staring at the city down the hill. She still had to figure out where she was going to stay the night. She didn't want dark to catch her without a safe room.

The feeling of being watched again twisted her stomach.

She had to be careful. She had to be smart. There was no telling what waited for her ahead.

TWO

MATT LADEL WOKE with a start as the alarm from his computer security room beeped loudly, echoing through his penthouse apartment.

At first, he couldn't figure out exactly what he was hearing. He had been dreaming about waking up in the morning in his old college dorm room, to his old alarm clock, and the dream had morphed into a nightmarish feeling of the alarm clock going off forever while he searched and searched for it under ten foot deep piles of clothes and stacks of books that seemed to stretch to the ceiling. He couldn't find it, no matter how hard he tried.

And the stupid ringing kept going and going.

He had lived that damned dream more times than he wanted to remember back in his college days. Now, years later, the dream still haunted him.

He needed to wake up, get out of the nightmare.

The reality of its high-pitched, quick-beat alarm slowly replaced the old ringing alarm in the dream. He opened his eyes and stared at the white ceiling and wood beams over his head.

College was long over, a thing of the dead past.

Something had triggered his security alarm again.

"Damn deer," he said, tossing aside the sheet, and standing. He was nude, but since the morning seemed hot and bright outside the windows, he didn't even bother to slip on his robe or slippers. He moved across the soft carpet toward the computer room, trying to push the sleep and the dream back completely.

College was gone, his friends were gone, and he was one of only a few people left alive. And if he ever found that old alarm of his from college, he'd smash it into a hundred pieces, just with the hopes that stupid dream would stop.

Outside the expanse of tall windows in his penthouse apartment, the sun had already cleared off the summer haze, and he could tell without even going out that the air was hot and dry. In the distance, Mt. Hood towered into the sky, snow still covering most of its peak. To his left, Mount St. Helens was smoking again. It had been doing that off and on for years, rebuilding itself from the huge explosion back in the eighties.

The penthouse apartment covered the entire thirty-second floor of the Baxter building. He had set it up to cater to his every need. It had soft, rich carpet, big expansive rooms, and an island kitchen in the center of the main room with bright lights and every appliance known. He loved cooking, and used the kitchen almost more than any other area.

He had picked the apartment because it was a completely defensible place to live. He had locked all the staircases and they could be easily blocked at three different levels. He had gotten an elevator working and he controlled it as well from the top floor. He had even installed a tight cable from his roof to the roof of another nearby building to use as an escape if something trapped him in the building, like a fire.

He had furnished the living room with a deep, comfortable recliner placed directly in front of a large screen television. He had also brought in a couch for the times he wanted to just lay down. To the right of the living room, he had put together a weight and exercise room to keep his six-foot frame in top shape. He lifted weights every day, and ran on a treadmill facing the windows. He figured that he would never know when being in top shape would save his life.

Another recliner sat in front of a massive picture window overlooking Portland and the Willamette River. It matched the one in the living room only because there had happened to be two of them in the furniture store the morning he had been looking, and they both fit into the bucket of his little tractor that he used to haul things around.

He loved just sitting in that chair with a drink in his hand staring at the mountains. Sometimes, he sat in the chair and read when it rained, watching the patterns of the water on the glass between chapters. When the rest of humanity had still been alive, he never would have been able to afford a place like this. Now, he figured he deserved it.

Besides, who could tell him no?

The loud beeping of the alarm continued, drawing him toward the computer room he had installed in the west corner room of the big penthouse. He had been an electrician before everyone had died. He had installed security cameras for a living for River Drive Security and Alarms. In fact, he had been installing a bank camera with his boss and two others the day everyone just keeled over dead. He and Jenkins had been down in the vault when suddenly everything went silent on the comm link with the boss in the truck.

Jenkins had gone up to investigate, leaving Matt in the vault. Matt had never seen him again. Matt had no doubt Jenkins was alive somewhere, but where was another question.

By the time Matt had given up waiting, left the vault open, and went to investigate, Jenkins was gone, and everyone else was dead.

Everyone.

Just killed instantly in the middle of whatever they were doing.

Matt had freaked, to say the least.

At first he thought it was something airborne that had killed everyone, and it would soon get him, so he had gone back inside the bank. But after a short time of staring at dead bank customers and tellers, his brain kicked in and he knew that staying in there was stupid. If it were something airborne, he would have been dead with everyone else.

Clearly, something about the big bank vault had protected him and Jenkins. He just didn't know from what.

For most of that first day, he had wandered the streets in shock, staring at bodies, not really heading anywhere in particular. After a while, he took to turning off the idling cars, reaching past bodies to yank out keys.

Slowly, as the day wore on, and no one came into the city to start rescue operations, and no planes circled overhead, it began to dawn on him that maybe he, and Jenkins, wherever he had gone, were the only ones left alive in a very large area.

Then, as Matt was turning off an idling car that had ended up against a light pole, he thought of his parents in the resort town of Bend. Had whatever caused this been larger than just the Portland area?

Suddenly, it had become important to him to find out just how widespread this disaster had been.

Bend was a little resort city over the Cascade Mountains at the foot of Bachelor Ski Area. He had managed to make the normal six-hour drive to Bend in just under twelve hours, using four different cars. When he came upon areas of the road that were so jammed with wrecks that he couldn't get around, he would simply leave the car he had been using, and hike until he found another usable car on the other side of the blockage.

He had hoped that his parents had been outside the influence of what had happened, but the closer he got to their home, the more he knew that they had not.

He found his parents both dead, as well as everyone else in the small town.

For an hour that night, he had sat in the middle of the main intersection, with the light changing from green to red over his head, honking a car's horn.

The sound seemed impossibly loud, echoing off the buildings and the pine-covered mountains.

No one came and told him to stop.

He knew right then and there that he was alone. Really alone, and the thought scared him more than he had ever been scared before.

The next few days were only a blur of memory and nightmare.

He had somehow managed to bury his parents next to his grandparents in the cemetery. Then he had gone down to his favorite bar and dragged all the bodies out onto the sidewalk and sat them at tables he had put there, posing each body as best he could in positions of drinking. He had figured if they died drinking, then they may as well spend eternity drinking.

Then he had gone inside, alone in the empty bar,

filled the top of the bar with bottles of booze from the bar's storeroom, and sat down on a stool. That day, and for a number of days after, he had gotten so drunk he couldn't think.

Finally, a nasty hangover and the smell of death drove him away from the small town and out into a cabin in the Cascade Mountains. He stayed in that cabin, pretending everything was just fine, for a long winter.

When he hiked back into Bend the next spring, he knew for a fact he could no longer pretend it all hadn't happened. He hadn't been dreaming and he hadn't gone crazy.

It had happened.

For the next year, he had wondered the Northwest, going from Seattle to Boise to Salt Lake, over to Sacramento, and then back up, looking for anyone else alive. He had run across a number of people, all coping with the death in one fashion or another. None of them were the types of people he wanted to stay with, even though some of them were friendly and happy to see him.

Finally, he had returned to Portland two years ago and set up his penthouse apartment.

Now his computer alarm kept beeping, getting louder as he entered the room he had set up for security.

"All right, all right," he said, "I'm coming. Damn deer, anyway."

He expected to see nothing on the monitor, and to have to rewind a recording to see what had triggered the alarm. He had set up the system of motion detectors two years ago right after moving into the penthouse. The sensors triggered cameras, and ran off of batteries that he exchanged and recharged every six months. He recorded the camera feeds in a bank of recorders here in the apartment.

He had installed the system when he realized the lights from his apartment could be seen for miles around the city at night. In fact, from across the river, his place stood out like a beacon.

He figured it would be better to know when someone else alive was getting close enough to see him. The cameras, waiting with motion detectors, guarded over twenty different ways into the main area of the city, and the entire area around his building.

"Stop it, already," he said aloud, dropping his nude body into the chair in front of his monitor command screens. He punched off the loud, annoying alarm, sighing at the sudden silence around him.

Then he glanced at the big control board map of the city. It filled one entire wall of the room. He had green and red lights showing the location of each of his motion detectors and cameras. A red light showed on the old Interstate 5 headed south in the Twiliger Curves area. Deer often went through there, since that area was between the hills and the river. And every year, since the disaster, the deer seemed to be getting more plentiful.

He flicked up an image from a camera he had hidden on a pole, expecting to see either deer, or nothing at all. The sight of a woman, standing on an overpass shocked him to his very core.

His fingers fumbled over the controls for a moment before he brought up the zoom.

A woman standing there by herself.

A very attractive woman.

It wasn't possible.

Yet there she stood.

THREE

THE HOT WIND WHIPPED around Carey, brushing the trees nearby, drying the sweat to her skin as she walked down the freeway on-ramp and moved around some wrecks, working her way toward the center of the city.

"I sure don't miss this heat. How can anyone live in this?"

She laughed. "Oh, yeah, I forgot, no one does."

These days she talked a lot to herself and her cats. It broke the silence. Often she had tapes and CDs playing while she worked or read. But mostly, she just talked to herself.

Sometimes, she actually cracked herself up. There sure wasn't anyone else to laugh at her stupid jokes.

So far, she had been traveling for three days from her home on the coast. She might have done it a little quicker, but she had been careful, taking her time and doing a little exploring along the eighty-mile trip. She hoped to be back to the coast within ten days total, which meant three days into the city, three back, leaving her four days to explore her old hometown. She had figured her cats would be all right for ten days.

She sure hoped they would be. They had enough food for a month, yet she worried about them.

Twice between here and her home, she had come across other live people, all from a distance. One man and a woman had sat on their porch and just watched her walk by, the man holding a rifle across his lap. Those two had looked the sanest of the people she had seen so far, and she had had no desire to talk to either of them.

Once she had had to hide from what appeared to be an insane man, walking along talking to himself. She could smell him from a hundred yards. Granted, civilization was gone, but bathing was something still easy to do. In fact, it was one of the more enjoyable things to do. She could spend hours in a hot bath with a good book and a glass of wine.

She used to cover the same eighty-plus miles between the coast and the city in a car in two hours. Back then, she would have never dreamed of walking that route. Of course, back then she would have never imagined doing some of the things she had done over the past three years to survive.

Mostly, she hadn't let herself think about the day everyone died. No point. Now, being back here in the city, she pretty much didn't have that choice. She was going to walk right back into the middle of those horrible memories.

Purposefully.

"Such a brave little girl," she said, and then laughed.

At times, she had trouble wrapping her mind around the fact that the world really was gone, yet she was one of the few still here. Back when she had lived and worked in the city, she had thought nothing of jumping in the car and heading to her parent's small beach home on the coast for a weekend, or even just dinner and a show at the casino. But now, for this trip back to the city, it had taken her a year to actually get up the nerve to leave the beach.

Damn, she missed her cats.

She adjusted one strap slightly so that it didn't rub her shoulder too long in the same position. The backpack contained enough water to get her by for a few days, changes of clothes, food for a week, and extra ammunition for her rifle and the pistol in her belt.

She had spent a good amount of time over the last two years learning how to fire that pistol and rifle quickly and accurately. The need for it had come clear one afternoon when she had gone down to the closest grocery store to haul out another load of canned food. Before she had gotten there, she had heard a man laughing. Then he had started firing round after round from a pistol into car windshields in the parking lot.

The guy had been clearly crazy, and Carey had managed to stay hidden and watch him for most of the day until he headed north on the coast highway.

That afternoon, she had found herself a pistol, and the next day the rifle. Now she considered herself a good shot with them, but had no way of really knowing, and she sure didn't want to test the theory on anything living.

As she moved in and around wrecked cars, she still couldn't shake that feeling of being watched. There was someone out there, of that she had no doubt. Whether or not they would show themselves was another matter.

She did a quick check to make sure the rounds were in place in the rifle, and then snapped a bullet into the chamber.

Her hope, and her fear, was there *would* be other survivors in the city. Hope for a community of them, with enough good people to have conversations. Fear that all the people she would find would be in a gang of thugs who would try to take her and make her a slave or something movie-horrid like that.

She had had the discussion between hope and fear many times over dinner with her cats. She was convinced that a normal, sane person would have given up hope of a real society reforming by now, but still, here she was today, standing on the edge of the city, ready to look for one.

Risking her life in the search.

Did that mean she was insane like some of the people she had seen alive? She didn't want to think she might be, even though she always talked to herself. She didn't feel insane, but then, does an insane person know she is insane?

A question for the century.

She would sometimes lay awake at night listening to the waves pound the beach and rocks below her home and worry about the answer to that deep question.

And then she would worry that wondering about such a question made her sane or insane.

The cats offered no answers.

On still other nights, she would lay in bed thinking of people, and how nice it would be to talk to someone, or even listen to someone. Just have companionship. Those nights often ended up in nightmares, or no sleep.

Other nights, after a long hot bath and a few glasses of wine, her mechanical, battery-powered friends helped her fall asleep. She liked those nights the best since the dreams were often of her old fiancée Paine and his wonderful smile on a naked Brad Pitt body.

But during the day, the constant question about

being the only sane person left alive haunted her like a ghost.

She knew how to be alone, how to live alone. Actually, she had gotten very good at it. But for some reason, the thought of dying old and alone scared her a great deal.

That final argument was what had gotten her out of the house and on this trip. The fear of dying alone and the desire to find people to talk to were the reasons she was here. She just had to keep that firmly in mind.

The memory of Paine's face flashed back to her, and she found herself smiling as she walked. Paine had been the man she had hoped to marry, spend the rest of her life with. He had been funny and had had a grin that could make a person just laugh at its silliness.

And he had loved her, something that made her feel lucky every day they had been together.

Even with everyone alive, she had been a loner of sorts, and except for Paine, and his wonderful smile, and green eyes, she might have stayed a loner, surrounded by millions of very-much-alive people. So some of this desire to find others made no real sense for her.

Still, even a loner needed company at times. It seemed, now was one of those times.

Around her, the dead city closed in on the freeway as she got closer and closer to the downtown area.

Nothing but the wind and the dust moved.

Oh, yeah, she was going to find Mr. Right here.

She laughed.

Sure thing.

FOUR

OVER THE LAST FEW YEARS, the only women he had seen at all had been with rough-looking men. Three different couples that he knew of lived in the surrounding areas around Portland, but none of them Matt wanted anything to do with, and he was sure they felt the same about him.

This was not one of those women.

This woman wore a black, sleeveless tee shirt, jeans, and tennis shoes. She had long brown hair pulled back tight, light skin, and a clearly muscled body.

He leaned forward, trying to get closer to the screen. He couldn't take his gaze off of her. In the last two years, he would have never expected to see a beautiful woman.

Hell, any single woman.

He watched as she jumped back off the concrete railing and dug into her backpack.

He stared as she wiped down her face and arms and then put on more suntan lotion. Clearly, she could sense that he was watching her, as she kept looking around her at all times.

He suddenly realized that she was a woman he

would have been attracted to when everyone was still alive.

How was that possible that she was now standing there on the freeway?

Alone.

He had had a number of steady girlfriends before everyone died. He had just broken up with Sunni the week before everything happened. Sunni had been a short, blonde Swedish-type from Southern California. They had met in a bookstore out in the Tigard area. She was working for Hewlett Packard, doing something she could never quite explain to him.

After six months, they had both just grown tired of each other, even though the sex had been great. He had no idea if she had survived. The chances weren't good, and it hadn't occurred to him to even go looking for her body where she worked.

He had kept the idea of ever meeting a decent woman again so tucked away in his mind, he wasn't sure yet if he was still dreaming. He had to be dreaming; yet he knew he wasn't.

Yet he had to be.

"Wake up, Matt old buddy!"

His voice echoed off all the equipment.

All right, he was awake. That meant that woman out there was real. Very real.

As he watched, she put a water bottle away, picked the backpack up, and slipped it on her shoulders. Then, with the rifle in her hand, she headed off the overpass, walking with the assured gait of someone who had confidence to spare.

"Wait!" he shouted at the screen. "I'm right here. "Don't go!

He wanted to watch her some more.

He wanted to meet her.

He wanted to talk to her.

It took only a moment before she was off the overpass and headed down the freeway toward town and out of that camera's range.

The moment she disappeared, he felt a jolt of panic go through him. "Oh, damn."

His hands scrambled over the massive control board he had set up for the security cameras. Finally, he managed to activate the next camera covering a section of the old Interstate 5 south of town.

For a long moment, he thought he had lost her. Then she came around a large pile-up of wrecked cars and kept walking, right at him, as again the motion alarm for that camera started to ring.

She was too good to be true.

An impossible dream.

Small, strong, confident, and good looking. Something had to be wrong with her.

He flipped off the alarm, sitting back in silence as he watched her stride toward him. She had the walk of someone in control, of someone not afraid of where she was heading. She was a survivor who looked like she lived alone.

This could not be happening.

Almost all of the human population of the planet seemed to be dead, yet here was a woman walking right into his life.

Or maybe through his life.

That thought scared him again. He couldn't just let this dream walk by. He had to do something.

But what? He had no idea where she was headed, what her experiences were over the last few years, if she even wanted to talk to anyone else.

And just like all the women he was attracted to back in his college days, he had no idea how to meet her.

The rifle she carried with ease seemed to grow bigger with every second. The way she handled it, and by the way she had a pistol tucked into her belt, she knew how to shoot.

She might just kill anything that came close to her and wonder why later.

He had no idea how to approach her.

At least back in college, trying to meet a girl didn't mean risking getting shot.

But as he stared at this woman's face as she got closer to his camera, he had no doubt that getting shot was a risk he was going to have to take.

FIVE

CAREY KEPT HER PACE SLOW and easy in the hot sun as she headed down the freeway, moving in and around wrecked cars. In every car the driver was still strapped behind the wheel, smiling skeleton-smiles at her. Human skeletons were just so much a part of the landscape; she had stopped noticing them a couple years ago. With skeletons and human bones being everywhere, they seemed unreal, almost plastic and sometimes comical, like bad special effects of an old movie, even though she knew deep down inside that every one of them had been a real person, with a real life.

Now, the worry she felt about going back into the city today had her noticing everything, and looking at everything with a cold eye of reality, including all the bodies.

"This ain't no movie, Carey. Stay alert."

He voice echoed off the hot concrete and then was taken by the warm wind. She stared ahead at the big overpass and the signs directing traffic to either the downtown area, or along the bridge and beyond to Seattle.

Seattle.

Wow, that seemed so far away to her. Maybe if there was no community of people here that she could meet, she could take a look in Seattle some day.

Maybe.

"And cows fly."

Her voice again echoed on the hot pavement. Seattle was too far away, too much to think about right now. She needed to focus on the city in front of her.

Portland seemed so familiar, yet so alien, especially walking along the freeway to get into town. She had driven this road a thousand times, but never walked it. No one ever walked along a freeway when the world was still pumping. Not and live very long anyway.

While walking, she noticed things she would never have time to see at sixty miles per hour. Pavement colors, buildings, the way signs were secured to the ground. All kinds of strange and useless things. And even though she didn't have to, she found herself staying to the road's edge more than she needed to, just out of respect for old habits.

On the day she had left three years ago, the city still had a sound of a few car motors running, of stoplights clicking as they changed, of power humming through the buildings and overhead lines.

Today, the city had no sound. Only the wind rustling the weeds and the birds chirping broke the silence. Cities were *supposed* to have sounds. Honking horns, construction noises, and police sirens. Not even in the middle of the night was a city ever really silent.

This city was deathly silent.

"This is creepy."

She could just turn around go home right now. What difference would it make?

She kept walking. Her mother's voice echoed in her head. *Such a brave little girl.*

Sometimes she wished she could get her mother to just shut up.

Carey moved under the freeway sign leading her toward the downtown and riverfront areas. She had better start figuring out exactly where she was heading, at least make the decision as to where she would spend the night. It would take some time to get a place comfortable enough to stay in.

Why hadn't she made that decision, had a plan, before now? Had she figured she would never get this far? Most of the time, her way of dealing with something stressful had been to just not think about it. Clearly, staying somewhere in the city had been one of those things.

She left the freeway and moved down onto Front Street, walking in the middle of the street instead of getting anywhere near the sidewalks. The sidewalks felt too close to the buildings to be safe at the moment.

Ahead of her, a dozen blocks or so, the Marriott Hotel tower rose over the river. She could stay there, in one of the unoccupied suites with a view of Mt. Hood and the river. When living here, she had never had a reason, or enough money, to stay in such a nice place. It would be a treat.

"A reward for finishing a long walk."

Her words echoed off a large pile-up of cars and the concrete of the overpass behind her.

She nodded to herself; glad she now had a plan. She would find a good room there, set it up as a base for exploring around the city. She would stock it with food; maybe even get a portable generator in for electricity. But before anything, she would have to check the water, to make sure the water tanks of a place like that had enough good water to last her for a time. In so many buildings, the water supply had been completely drained. Water would make her final decision for her when she got there. After a day in this hot sun, she was going to need a shower. Maybe two.

With a little work, she could even make whatever place she found permanent.

"Duh, why not?" It hadn't occurred to her until just that moment that she could have a place in the city, a place on the coast, a place just about anywhere in the world she wanted.

Nothing was stopping her.

No one was stopping her.

All she would have to do is figure out a way to move her cats from one home to the next with her.

She moved along Front Street. A dozen more blocks and she would be at the hotel. The grass along the river to her right had turned to weeds; the sidewalks and streets were cracked and growing grass in places. Still, the city had a beauty about it, with the blue river flowing through it, the mountains around it, and the green trees everywhere.

The air smelled faintly of water and fish, and birds chirped and flitted from nests in the branches of the trees along the old riverside park. She could see where birds had stained the edges of buildings and built nests in windows. It was lucky she had come into town on such a beautiful day. Even if this trip was a waste of time, it was at least replacing the images of her last days here with something more pleasant.

Two blocks short of the hotel, something moved out of the corner of her eye. She snapped around, the rifle up and aimed, her blood racing. The feeling of being watched had suddenly returned stronger than ever.

A bird flittered away.

She sighed and lowered the gun.

"All right," she said out loud, letting her voice slow her racing heart, "Calm down and don't go shooting everything that moves."

"I'm very glad to hear you say that," a deep, rich voice said to her left.

She spun around, the rifle up again.

Every nerve, every ounce of focus was on the rifle and her finger and where she was aiming it.

She found herself face-to-face with a man about her age, with brown, unruly short hair, twinkling brown eyes, and a large smile. He had his hands in the air like he had just been caught robbing a bank.

She tried to take a breath and failed as she stared at him.

He had moved out of the shadows near an office building and now was standing no more than fifteen steps from her. He wore a plain white tee shirt, jeans and new-looking tennis shoes. He had the appearance of having dressed quickly, yet still seemed together and clean.

Very clean.

Tanned.

Healthy.

She bet he even smelled good.

And he was one of the best-looking men she had ever seen, even before everyone died.

It was as if time in the dead city around them froze.

Nothing on the street moved.

The river sounds seemed to drop back to silence.

She didn't even feel the heat, couldn't hear the birds.

She kept her gaze locked on his, the rifle pointed at his chest. She had hoped to find someone else alive and sane, but she had never expected to.

And she had never expected to find someone so good-looking.

She just hoped she wouldn't have to shoot him.

The seconds seemed to go on forever as she drank in this man, memorizing every detail.

"I'm not going to bite," the guy said, smiling. His voice was deep and rich and matched his rugged face.

She was surprised his voice stayed level and didn't shake, even though she could tell he was worried about her putting a hole in his chest. She doubted anything intelligent at all could come out of her mouth at the moment.

He laughed. "Sorry for the cliche. I didn't know what else to say. As you can see, I am unarmed and alone."

Then he shrugged.

She didn't lower her gun, and he didn't lower his arms.

She had to get her wits about her, really find out who this person was, and what she had just walked into.

Was this a trap? Was he the bait to get her guard down so others could overwhelm her?

They stared at each other for a few long seconds, then she decided to try to speak. She swallowed and then managed to get the words out.

"How did you know I was here?"

She was proud that she had made the question sound authoritative, and that not a word broke.

"Security cameras," he said, pointing up at the top of a pole back down Front Street. "I have them on all the main entrances into town. A person living alone in the big city can never be too careful."

He smiled at her, and then went on. "But to be honest, I was also hoping to find someone else alive, passing through."

"And you sit all day and watch your cameras?" she asked, now even more worried that she had run into another weirdo. Why hadn't she listened to her little voice when she felt she was being watched? She should have just turned around, found another way into the city. Mistakes like that could get her killed.

He laughed. "Hardly. In fact, you woke me when you stopped on the overpass. I have motion detector alarms with each camera."

She could feel herself starting to relax just a little, and her little voice wasn't screaming that this man was dangerous like some of the others she had seen alive. She would have set up security cameras like he described if she had thought of it, or known how. Especially living in a big city area where a lot of people would naturally go through.

She kept her rifle aimed at him and forced herself to think, slowly, giving herself time to calm down.

One mistake, one slip, and she could find herself in a very bad situation. He was shorter than Paine had been, but still clearly very strong. She had to be careful, no matter how much she wanted to lower her gun and hug this stranger and talk to him.

"So, where do you live?" she asked.

"Baxter building," he said, indicating with one raised hand the direction of the main part of town.

"Been there for two years, in the penthouse. How about you?"

"I've been on the coast," she said, feeling that even that small amount of information was too much. At least she hadn't told him which part of the coast.

He nodded, as if understanding that. "Yeah, I was up in the Cascades, in the forest, until the smell cleared."

"Are you alone?" she asked.

"Yeah," he said.

She was thrilled, for some reason, at that news, but at the same time, it made her even more worried about him. She was going to have to put aside her attraction for this man, and her desire to talk to him, and think clearly.

Hard to do. He was so fantastically good-looking. And those eyes of his just begged to be stared into.

"How did you survive?" she asked.

"I was doing the security system in a bank in Beaverton when all this happened. I was down in the vault, but I have no idea why that protected me. Or even what happened to everyone."

"I do," she said.

At that his eyes lit up, and his arms lowered a little. "You do? Why? How? I mean, if you know that, if you would tell me what happened to everyone, it would help me figure out where there are more people alive."

She took her first deep breath since she had been surprised by this hunk of a man, and ignored his question for a moment. Clearly, if he had been watching her, he had known she had a rifle, had known she would get the drop on him, and had risked being shot by introducing himself.

Either the guy had courage, and really wanted her to trust him.

Or he was stupid beyond words.

Or he was working some other trick on her, and had friends helping him trap her.

She glanced around.

Her back was to the riverbank. There was no way anyone could come up behind her where they were standing.

"I'm alone, honest," he said, noticing her movement. Again he shrugged. "I wish I wasn't, to be honest with you. But not many people around here left to talk to these days."

"No groups?"

"None," he said. "A few couples living out on the outskirts of town, but they're not friendly. And the last guy to go through town that I saw was talking to himself, dragging a kid's wagon, and carrying machine guns. I didn't talk to him."

"So in all of this main part of the city, you're it?"

He spread his arms wider over his head and smiled. "I'm the entire population of downtown Portland, Oregon. And considering my cameras and security system, I would know if anyone else was around."

She said nothing to that, wondering how much she could trust this guy who was clearly trying to show her he could be trusted. Even back when everyone was still alive, she didn't trust too many people, so trust would take a while with this guy. At least she didn't have to keep her gun trained on the only person she had talked to in three years.

She motioned that he should lower his arms, and she lowered the rifle, keeping her finger beside the trigger and the rifle ready to bring back up quickly.

"Thanks," he said. He moved his shoulders around a few times. "I clearly need more reps on those hand-raising isometrics."

She smiled, and he smiled back.

God, she loved his smile. How could one of the last men alive on Earth have such a wonderful smile?

"So, do you have a name?" she asked.

"Matt," he said. "Matt Landel. An actual, native Oregonian, born and raised."

She actually laughed at that, the sound echoing over the river. Being native was something that mattered only to Oregonians. She liked the name, and she liked how it sounded coming from his mouth. So far, she liked a lot about what she saw with this guy. And that worried her.

"I'm Carissa Noack. People used to call me Carey. Also a native, through and through."

It felt strange using her full name after all the years. Strange, and yet somehow normal, as if having and using a full name returned a little civilization to the world.

He smiled at her. "Nice meeting you, Carey."

"Nice to meet you as well, Matt," she said.

Then the silence of the city pounded back in on her as they stood like two high school kids at a dance wondering who was going to make the first move.

"How about I cook us both breakfast?" Matt said, finally breaking the silence with a rushed sentence. "My stomach is starting to sound like an earthquake coming, and I bet you haven't had a good omelet since you left the coast."

"Omelet?" she asked, the word out of her mouth before she had a chance to stop it. She hadn't had anything like a real egg since she moved to the coast. On the hike in, she had seen chickens, but she hadn't been able to get close to any.

"Yeah, real eggs and everything," he said. "Honest."

"How? Here in the city?"

He nodded, smiling as if he were very proud of having eggs. "It seems chickens survived whatever killed everyone. So I went out into the country and trapped some, including roosters, and set them loose in the Rose Garden."

"You're kidding?" she asked. The Rose Garden was the big basketball arena where the Portland Trailblazers had played.

"I'm not," he said, laughing again.

His laugh just made her smile, and relax even more, even though she didn't want to.

"I figured the seats would make great nests for them, plus it's big enough to hold a lot of birds and give them room to move around, but not escape."

She laughed at the idea of The Rose Garden as a giant chicken coop. How perfect. "What do you feed them? How many do you have?"

He shrugged. "Every few weeks I scatter a pickup truck load of grain from sacks I found in a warehouse down by the river. Every month or so I trap some more birds and turn them loose in there. The population seems to be growing, but in a place that size it's hard to count. I try to go get the eggs I can find every few days and there are always more than I can use. I take a bird or two every few weeks for special dinners. I bet I have five hundred birds now, if not more."

"Amazing," she said.

"Thanks," he said, smiling. "I'd be glad to show it to you, right after breakfast. I make a great omelet, honest.

And I would love to have someone to talk to while I'm cooking after all these years."

She stared at him for a moment. She had come back into town with the hope of finding someone else still alive. Now she had, and she didn't know what to do. She hadn't expected this, she hadn't expected anyone, let alone a great-looking guy who could raise chickens and claimed he could cook.

She had to keep her guard up, stay alert, watch herself.

And if he turned out to be as nice as he seemed, then she would cross that bridge when it was proven to her. But that was going to take some time.

She was about to agree to go with him for breakfast, like a bad pick-up at closing time in a bar, when her voice in her head screamed at her.

What was she thinking?

She took a deep breath and stared into his eyes. She couldn't just go up into a strange man's penthouse apartment and have breakfast. She wouldn't have done that back when the world was still alive.

Why was she thinking of doing that now? Had three years of being along, taking baths with mechanical toys, made her that desperate?

The answer was yes.

But that didn't matter. The danger was too great.

"I think I'd better wait on that," she said.

The look of disappointment on his face was clear to her, but he nodded. "I understand. I wouldn't trust anyone in these circumstances either. Especially someone I just met. Sorry, don't know what I was thinking."

"It was a nice offer," she said. "Maybe I'll take a rain check."

He indicated the beautiful, cloudless sky above them, and then with a smile said, "I hope you don't decide to wait until it actually rains."

"We'll see," she said, smiling back.

"So where are you thinking of staying?" he asked. "You are staying for at least the night, aren't you?"

She nodded. She could trust him enough to tell him that, since he had cameras and more than likely could follow her anyway. "Marriott," she said. "It seemed a logical place to set up a camp and look around."

"Water's all drained out of the building system," he said, shaking his head. "But the last time I was in the Embassy Suites it seemed to have water. Nicer place, too."

She nodded. The Embassy Suites was the old Multnomah Hotel that had been remodeled years back into large suites. She had been inside it only once, and had been impressed.

"Thanks," she said. "I'll try there then."

"There's a decent hardware store about two blocks west of there that might have some portable generators," he said. "I'll be glad to help you get set up if you like."

They stood there, in the street, staring at each other, letting his question hover in the warm air. She really didn't want to take her gaze off of this man, yet she knew she had to move, give herself time to think, make sure she was safe.

"Thanks," she said. "I might take you up on that. But first I just sort of want to look around. Haven't been here in three years."

He nodded. "You know where I live if you need anything," he said, pointing around and up at the Baxter building. "Just go into the lobby and I'll know you're there."

With that he smiled; clearly embarrassed he had told her that piece of information about his security system.

"How about we meet for lunch tomorrow?" she said, not wanting to have any chance slip past that she would get to talk to this man again. Of course, if she stayed in town, he was the only man or person she could talk to.

"Name the time, name the place," he said, his eyes not hiding the fact that he liked her idea. "I'll bring a picnic basket full of fried chicken."

She laughed at that, wondering just how wonderful fried chicken was going to taste after three years of eating mostly fish.

"How about outside the used and rare room in Powells Bookstore? Have you been up there?"

"I have," he said. "That sounds perfect. Big windows, tables and chairs. I'll even bring a tablecloth and plates."

"Twelve noon?" she asked.

"Twelve noon it is," he said. "Right now my watch says it's just after ten in the morning."

"So does mine," she said, glancing at the watch she'd been wearing for years. She couldn't remember the last time she had actually looked at it for any reason other than to check how long it would be until the sun went down.

"Tomorrow then," he said. "I'm looking forward to it. And my offer stands, if you need help, just come to the lobby of the Baxter building."

"Thanks," she said. "I really appreciate that."

He turned and went back the way he had come, stepping into the shadows of the building and disappearing.

Had she just imagined all that?

Did she really have a date tomorrow?

She looked around at the dead city, the wrecked cars, the skeletons in the driver's seats, and just shook her head.

Post-apocalyptic dating. How much stranger could things get?

SIX

MATT COULD NEVER have imagined, when he crawled out of bed that morning to shut off the stupid alarm, that he would feel so much like a high school kid again.

He walked down the sidewalk, heading back toward the Baxter building, trying not to whistle. Not once, since the world ended, had he felt so good, so light, so positive about any future. Not only had she told him she knew what had happened to everyone, but she had agreed to see him again.

And it had been her idea on how to meet.

He hadn't been this excited, and this scared, for a long, long time.

Back when he was a junior in high school, he had wanted to ask one of the cheerleaders, Betty Rees, to the fall formal. It had taken all of his courage, and some pushing by his best friend, Dave, to finally approach her.

Matt was, as they liked to be called around school, one of the "ghosts." He never really did much in sports, so he wasn't a jock, and his grades were just okay, so he wasn't a brain. And he didn't hang out with any of the known groups such as the science geeks, the band, the skateboarders, or the druggers. He was a ghost, just there, going to school, not really noticed.

Why he had ever thought Betty would say yes to him was beyond imagining now. At least she hadn't laughed at him when he asked.

Then she had done the unthinkable and said, "I'd love to."

It had taken him a moment to realize she had said yes, then for the next three weeks he had worried and fretted about it, especially when she stopped and talked to him in the halls, something she had very seldom done before.

The dance, what he remembered of it, had been fun. Terrifying and fun. She had even kissed him good-night, since he didn't have the courage back then to kiss her.

That night had made them friends, and they had remained that way right up to the day everyone was killed. Just friends, nothing more, which had been fine with him. She was always a cheerleader in his mind, and very scary.

Now this woman, Carey, had said she wanted to have lunch with him. Just talking to her had made him as nervous as talking to Betty in the hallway, and not because she was carrying a rifle.

Well, maybe a little because she was carrying a rifle.

But mostly because she was a good-looking woman that he was attracted to, in a world where most of the people had died. In this situation, doing the right thing and not making her mad was another level of stakes all-together.

Risking getting shot had been worth talking to her.

And even though she had turned down his stupid idea for breakfast, she had asked to see him again.

They had a date.

Noon tomorrow.

Lunch.

Now it felt like he was right back in high school, getting ready for the big dance with Betty.

He unlocked his security precautions in the Baxter building lobby, and used the elevator to get back to his apartment, even though most times he took the stairs because twenty-two flights of stairs gave him some good exercise. This morning he was in too good of a mood to climb stairs.

Even though his stomach was grumbling from lack of breakfast, he headed for the security room, grabbing a breakfast bar along the way. His battery-powered camera network around the city was pretty extensive. He wanted to make sure that if Carey got into trouble anywhere the cameras could see, he would know about it.

Or if she was out of range, at least have an idea where she had gone last.

Plus, he just wanted to see her again. He had to admit that. He wanted to know if she was real, as nice, as friendly as she seemed.

When he left this morning, he had turned off the security alarms, but left on the recording devices for the cameras. On his big board a big bunch of red lights showed where movement had happened.

The area in front of his building, of course, meaning it had recorded him going and coming. And the light on the area where he and Carey had talked was also blinking.

And three other lights in the areas Carey would

have gone through in heading toward the Embassy Suites.

He brought up the last section, just in time to see her look both directions along the street, and then go inside the old hotel.

Just the glimpse of her sent his heart racing and his stomach twisting. How could one woman do that to him?

He sat, staring for a moment at the door she had disappeared through. Finally, he said out loud as his stomach grumbled. "Come on, you can't just sit here all afternoon and watch for her."

He reset the alarms and headed for the kitchen. He needed some breakfast. He didn't need to watch for her. His motion sensors would tell him if she left.

Suddenly, he felt guilty spying on her, like he was some sort of peeping tom. He shook that thought off. He could be excused wanting to watch a beautiful woman, wanting to make sure she stayed safe.

Especially since she was one of the last beautiful women left alive in the world.

SEVEN

CAREY MOVED EASILY along Front Street, staying close to the river, her rifle in her hands. The sweat from her hands made the rifle feel slick, but she wasn't shouldering it until she got to a place she felt safe. And out here, in the open, next to the river, she didn't feel safe.

On each side street she passed that led up into the big buildings of the downtown area, she watched for Matt, expecting him to be pacing her.

He wasn't.

No movement, no sign of him at all.

Or of anyone else.

It took her six blocks of glancing over her shoulder and staring up each street to make sure he wasn't following. Part of her wanted him to, part of her was afraid he would. She was having trouble believing he was what he said he was, yet she had no reason to doubt him. He didn't let off that "danger" signal that she got from some men.

Her mother had told her to learn to trust that danger signal. And a couple times, trusting it had gotten her out of bad places back when she was in college.

Matt felt safe. Good point number one. He was interesting and funny, and incredibly good-looking, in that rugged way.

Good points two, three, and four.

His eyes were full of life, his smile made her smile just thinking of it, and his voice was deep and full enough that she wanted to just spend time listening to him talk.

She had lost count of his good points.

She had felt when meeting him just like she felt back in college, not knowing what to say, or what to do when having to talk to a strange man. Clearly, living on her own, and surviving the end of the world, hadn't given her any more confidence in that area. Actually, considering he was the first person she had actually talked to in three years, she had done all right.

What had amazed her was that he had taken such a risk in just meeting her. She doubted she would have stepped out of the shadows, unarmed, to meet someone she didn't know who had just wandered into her area. Yet he had done that, to make her feel safer. The man named Matt either had amazing courage, or amazing stupidity. From the light in his eyes, she would bet on the courage.

Meeting him tomorrow for lunch was just about as crazy on her part. But since he had taken a risk that she would shoot him on sight, she would take a risk having lunch with him.

She had moved on past the Marriott Hotel without stopping, making her way along the river toward the Burnside Bridge. From there, she knew how to find the Embassy Suites Matt had suggested.

She forced herself to keep her attention on where she was going, what was happening around her, instead of thinking about him. It was hard, but in these times, a daydream could get her killed.

The city was as dead, as silent as it had felt coming in. Only the birds and the warm wind broke the stillness. It seemed that Matt had been telling her the truth, that she really was the only one besides him in this area. She could see no evidence of anything, or anyone else. No worn trails, no looted stores, nothing but a dead city, frozen in time from a morning three years ago.

It took her a good fifteen minutes after her meeting with Matt, but she finally found the old Multnomah Hotel that had been remodeled into the Embassy Suites a decade before. The front of the old hotel faced a fairly empty side street, with a parking garage on the corner. A limo was pulled up out front, the driver still behind the wheel.

The doorman had slumped over a cart full of luggage, and his body had somehow stayed there through the winter storms.

With a quick look in both directions along the street, she decided to go in.

The front door stuck for a moment, then let her into a musty-smelling entrance area that contained five skeletons in different locations around the fairly small space. She went slowly up the two stairs and into the high-ceilinged main lobby area.

The carpet was a rich-looking red, and the artificial plants gave the room a feeling of luxury, even though it was coated with a layer of grayish dust.

The footprints in front of her on the carpet were clear. One of the sets of prints must have been Matt's, since he admitted being in here. Another set, bigger and with a wider stance, was from some time back, before Matt had come in.

There was no sign that anyone else had been in the building, at least through this entrance, at any time in the recent past.

She relaxed a little and slung her rifle over her shoulder, then dug out a flashlight and a water bottle. The room was cooler than outside, making her realize just how much she had been sweating. The light from the front windows was enough in the main room, but if she were going to head down a hallway, or climb stairs, she would need her flashlight.

She stood, looking around, studying the skeletons that slumped in the waiting area near what must have been their luggage. She could still remember waiting like that for a ride, or a bellman, or for someone to join her from a room. Who knew why these people had been waiting, but they still waited, now forever.

She finished a long drink and put the water bottle back in her backpack, then looked around at the exits. When finding rooms to stay at night on the trip from the coast to Portland, she had made sure she stayed on the main floor. She had figured that was safer. But now, here in this building, it might be safer for her to see what was on the upper floors before deciding. As long as she had two or three good ways out, she would be fine.

She went over to the front desk and crawled up on it, looking along the counter behind the desk for some sort of master key. With the power off, the door key-card systems in these big hotels reverted to a type of punch key that was always kept close by. It took her a minute, but she found it, then slid off the front desk and headed for the back.

She followed what she thought was Matt's tracks in the dust on the carpet to a stairwell, and then inside, she clicked on the flashlight. It seemed to be open all the way up, with no problems.

She used a chair to block open the door into the staircase at the bottom, just in case the door locked behind her. The last thing she needed was to get trapped in a staircase with no one left alive to find her.

Then she realized that wasn't the case. Matt knew where she was going. That thought both eased her fear a little, and worried her. She had spent three years doing just fine on her own. She didn't want to start making mistakes now, thinking she had a person backing her up. She didn't even really know him yet, and certainly didn't trust him.

She followed the tracks in the dust on the staircase all the way to the top floor, seven floors up. She tried to move slowly, carefully, to not kick up any more of the layer of dust than she needed to. The air in the stairwell was stuffy enough without adding swirling dust to it.

At the top, the old footprints went out into a hallway through an unlocked door. The narrow corridor was lit only by the windows on either end, but was bright enough for her to turn off her flashlight.

The footprints went to a window and vanished.

She followed them, then looked out the window. Beyond was a metal fire escape that led both up and down. It looked like Matt had forced the window open, then closed it behind himself after he went through.

The fire escape ladder led down to the top of the building beside the old hotel. This wasn't a way to the ground directly, but it was a good escape. So she had the staircase she had come up, the fire escape through the window. What other ways were there off this floor?

She opened a door labeled no admittance and

shined her flashlight into the dark area. Service elevator, but no staircase.

She went back to the elevator and stair area and looked down another side hall. There was another exit sign there, clearly leading to another staircase. She liked that. Three ways down.

She took the master key and faced the guest door closest to the elevator area in the same hallway as the window fire escape. It took her a moment, but the passkey finally clicked something and the door opened.

She took one look inside the large area and pulled the door closed, not going inside. The last guests were still at home, still in bed.

She moved down one door and opened it.

It had a made bed and no sign of anyone staying.

"Wow," she said, letting the door close behind her and moving into the large, multi-roomed suite. She moved across the main room and carefully pulled open the drapes, trying to stir up as little dust as possible while letting the sun fill the space.

The room had high ceilings, clearly left from its days as an old hotel. And from the looks of it, in the re-modeling they had combined at least three, maybe four of the old hotel rooms, into this suite. There was a small kitchen area, a large dining area, a business desk, and a room with a bed big enough for three or four people.

"Now the test," she said, moving into the tiled bathroom with old-fashioned gold faucets and a basket of soap. A bathrobe hung on the back of the door with a sticker saying it was free for guest use. This bathroom was larger than her old dorm room in college, and not only had a shower, but a huge step-up bathtub with what looked like special jets.

"Oh, baby, let this work."

She twisted the cold water on the sink faucet. For a moment nothing happened, but she could feel the air being shoved through the system. Then, with a loud sputtering sound, water came out, running dark and rust-colored, spitting with the air bubbles. It smelled like water that had sat for three years in pipes. She had expected as much. But at least it was flowing. Matt had been right.

She moved over to the bathtub and turned the faucet there. It too started running after a moment, filling the tub with nasty looking water.

She started the shower as well, then went back into the dining area and took off her pack. The release of the pressure on her back felt great. She had carried that pack so much over the past three days, it felt as if it were a part of her.

She laid her rifle on the table beside the pack, but kept her pistol in her belt. She wanted to do a little more looking around. She needed to leave tracks into every room on this floor in the dust in the hallway. If she stayed here long enough, she'd clean the dust completely out of the hallway, but for now, if she had been followed, she needed to make sure no one would come easily to this room.

She went back into the bathroom and checked the water. It was still flowing, and a lot better looking. Another ten minutes and she just might have clean enough water to take a shower in.

She looked longingly at the bathtub. If she got a generator up here, she could even heat some water for a warm bubble bath.

She went back out into the hall, blocking the suite door open so she wasn't separated from her pack, then used the master card to open every door and walk into each room on the floor, shuffling her feet as she moved along the hall.

Fifteen minutes of very dusty work later, no one, at a glance, could tell which room she was in. At last, she had a place to stay.

"One problem solved. Now to problem number two. Getting clean."

She went back into the suite, closed, locked, and blocked the door with a chair, then headed for the bathroom. A long, cold shower was going to feel very, very good.

And she did some of her best thinking in showers. After meeting Matt this morning, she had a lot of thinking to do.

EIGHT

MATT FINISHED his breakfast, then checked his security room to see if Carey had moved, even though he knew his alarms would have told him if she had.

Nothing.

Of course, she might have gone out the back. He didn't have security cameras in that area. But somewhere along the way, if she had left, she would trip one of his sensors and he would know.

He hoped she hadn't left, that she was what she had seemed to be, a survivor with a lot of guts, wanting to explore her old home town.

He dropped into his big chair and stared at the security screens showing the empty city around him. Now, the city didn't feel so empty. How one woman could make such a difference, he didn't know. But she sure had.

But now he had a problem. He had promised her fried chicken for their lunch tomorrow, but he didn't have a fresh chicken in his freezer. He needed to get out to the Rose Garden and get some fresh eggs and a chicken. At the same time, he didn't want to leave the security room in case she decided to move.

He wanted to watch her, protect her if she needed it, help her if she needed that.

What happened if she came to the Baxter building while he was gone and didn't find him. How would she trust him after that?

"Get it together, Matt. Leave her a note."

One on the outside door to the building, and another on the main staircase door, telling her where he had gone, what he was doing.

That felt like a silly thing to do, but he had no doubt, he would do it.

He sat, watching the monitors for any movement, planning a very special lunch for tomorrow. He wanted it to be special. After three years, the first meal with someone else demanded to be special.

Fried chicken and a chilled bottle of Chablis from the Willamette Vineyards. He needed to make a lot of chicken. Too much, actually. He wanted to give her pieces to pick from. And maybe two bottles of wine in case the conversation lasted as he hoped it would.

Her smile, the sound of her voice came back to him clearly. He wanted to very much make the lunch last, find out who she really was, let her know that he was safe and a friend.

What else needed to be in a picnic lunch? Fresh rolls. He could bake rolls tomorrow morning with the chicken, just before going. And, of course, deviled eggs. Deviled eggs always went great on a picnic, especially the ones he made, from his Aunt Rose's old recipe.

It felt like he was forgetting something.

He tried to remember back to the picnics he used to go on when he was a child, usually up on the shores of one of the lakes in the Cascades. His mother and grandmother always made the best picnics, and always brought them in those wicker baskets.

He'd search a few stores on the way back from the Rose Garden, see if he could find a wicker picnic basket. And he needed to bring plates, silverware, and napkins as well.

But he was forgetting something on the menu. He could feel it.

Deviled eggs, fried chicken, fresh rolls, and what?

The memory of sitting on a blanket on a warm July day on the shores of the lake came back strong. His dad had tied up their boat on the sandy beach and his mother was unloading the basket. Life had seemed so perfect back then, and actually, it was. He had had a great childhood, one of the best.

He let himself relive the memory.

First, she took out a big bowl of fried chicken, covered in tin foil. The wonderful smell was always enough to make Matt want to just grab a piece right then. Of course, she never let him, not until everyone was seated on the blanket.

Then she took out a plastic container filled with deviled eggs, then a plastic sack with corn-on-the-cob smothered in butter and wrapped in tin foil.

Corn. Of course, corn and Jell-O. His mom always included corn-on-the-cob and Jell-O. Half the time, the Jell-O had gotten near something that was hot, and had half melted. His mother was always annoyed at that and his dad always just laughed.

Matt didn't much care for the Jell-O, but he could do the fresh corn just fine. It was late enough in the season that his corn in his roof garden had fresh ears on them.

He had it. The perfect picnic lunch. And he would

get to Powell's early enough to do a little cleaning up there, wash a window so they would have some decent sunlight, wipe off a few tables and chairs.

The idea of having a picnic with Carey had him so excited, he doubted he was going to sleep much tonight.

"Okay, so much for meal planning," he said out loud, clicking off his audio alarms and leaving the system to record any movement in the city while he was gone. "Time to get everything ready."

He stood and headed for the door of the penthouse, grabbing a backpack to carry the eggs and chicken back in. He also picked up his rifle and a box of shells, slipping the shells into the pack. It was a habit he had always done while leaving, and this morning, being out in the city without a gun had felt damned strange. It had to be the first time he'd done that since moving back to the city.

The risk he had taken to meet Carey was amazing. She could have easily been insane and shot him. He was very glad she hadn't.

He made the two notes to Carey to stick on the building's doors, then started down the staircase, going at a slow but steady clip, thinking about the route he needed to take to get across the river to the Rose Garden.

Usually, he went within a few blocks of where she was staying and walked over the Burnside Bridge, but he didn't want to do that today. He didn't want to do anything to spook her, make her think he was dangerous in any way.

More than anything, he wanted her to show up tomorrow at Powell's.

He went through his lobby and outside, putting up the notes as he went. Then he turned straight downhill toward the river. He would use the Morrison Bridge and go around that way, away from the area Carey was in. A little farther to walk, and harder to get past a few wrecks, but worth not taking any chance at getting too close to where she was staying.

Portland had been a very big city while it was full of people. And a very big place when he was alone. Now, with Carey here, the city seemed frighteningly small.

NINE

THE COLD SHOWER felt wonderful as it washed off the sweat and dust from the long morning hike into the city. Carey had found the hotel's linen closet in the hallway and broke in, getting two fresh towels that hadn't been hanging up and weren't covered in dust. It was interesting how many tricks like that she had learned in the last few days, some from thinking a situation through, others from mistakes.

Learning about hanging towels had been a mistake on her first morning on this trip. She had managed to find a place with running water, taken a shower, then as if the maids had just left the towel on the towel rack, she took the closest one and started to dry herself, finding herself coated in dirt and mud almost immediately.

Gross, disgusting, and downright weird feeling. If it hadn't been so annoying, it might have been funny. Even though she was convinced no one was within miles of her, she had still used the muddy towel to wrap herself in while going in search of a clean towel. She had called herself "Mud Girl" the rest of the day.

She was getting better at picking places to stay as well. This bathroom had a decent-sized window, so there was even enough light for her to see what she was doing. The room she had found on the second night didn't have a window in the bathroom, and she had had to get ready and shower in the almost complete darkness.

She wondered as she dried off and dug out some clean clothes, if agreeing to meet Matt had been another mistake on this trip. Granted, there just weren't that many people left alive and she was hungry for company. And he seemed the same way. But even still, she had to be careful. There were no police, no parents, no friends left to come to her rescue if she got herself in a bad situation.

She finished dressing and moved over to one of the big windows that looked out over the buildings and the river. The room had stayed fairly cool, but she could tell that outside the temperatures were climbing. It was going to be a very hot day. She missed the coast, the cool breezes off the water, the summer fog.

And she missed her cats.

"Well, you made it here," she said out loud, her voice breaking the silence in the room. "Now what?"

She stood, staring out the window at the river, thinking about going to her old apartment. Paine's body would be there, in her bed. She wouldn't mind having a few of her old things from her place, but she just didn't feel up for going there yet.

Or to her parents' house over the hill in Beaverton. Maybe on the way out of town, on her way back to the coast, she would stop and see both places, pick up a few small things to take home, pay her respects to the three people she had loved the most in the world.

Or maybe she'd do that next trip. She wasn't sure if she had the emotional stability to see them just yet.

Some movement caught her eye on the Morrison Bridge. Someone was walking there.

She grabbed her binoculars from her pack and focused in on who it was.

Matt.

Even from a distance, her heart leaped at just seeing him again. He had what looked like an empty backpack on one shoulder and a rifle slung over the other. So he really had purposely come to see her unarmed earlier.

That made her feel a little better about him, a little safer about their lunch tomorrow. He had been willing to risk his life, something he clearly didn't normally do, just to meet her. Amazing, and a little bit stupid, actually.

She watched him pick his way along the bridge, through the wrecks.

"So, where are you going now, handsome fella?"

Suddenly, the answer dawned on her. He had promised her fried chicken and said his chickens lived trapped in the Rose Garden. He was going to get a chicken for their lunch.

She smiled, watching him move over the bridge and out of sight, feeling disappointed when she couldn't see him any more. She couldn't believe how smart he had been to put chickens in the Rose Garden. It gave him a constant source of food besides a garden, which she bet he had somewhere in the city as well.

Everything about him seemed smart, except his stunt this morning. He appeared nice and was very attractive. She would have thought that even if he wasn't one of the last people alive on the planet.

She was going to have to be careful. Very careful. And go very slowly with him. Clearly, around him, her judgement might not be what it should be.

She searched for him one more time along the far river bank, disappointed that she couldn't see him.

"Okay, better get this place livable," she said, turning away from the window and looking at the high-ceilinged room with its dining table, big soft chair, and huge bed and dresser.

She went back into the bathroom, got two towels damp and another clean towel from the stack she had taken from the linen closet, then slowly started wiping off the dust from every surface.

Then she went back to the linen closet and found clean sheets and a bedspread, taking the ones on her room's bed out and putting them in the service area.

Then she washed the insides of the main window, as high as she could reach. Amazing what a little sunshine can do for moods. Hers was getting better by the moment as she settled in.

Actually, she was almost dancing around doing the cleaning, and it wasn't from the sunlight. The idea of actually having lunch with another person had her so excited, she wasn't sure if she could wait until tomorrow.

But she knew she would.

She downed the last of her bottled water after finishing with as much cleaning as she could do with wet towels. Then she emptied out her backpack, took her pistol and some extra ammunition, and left the rest of her things in the room. She needed more bottled water and there was a drugstore on the corner that might have cases of the stuff.

She went down the other staircase exploring each floor as she went. Nothing out of the usual. And no other tracks in the dust.

She was right about the drugstore, it did have bottled water, along with a large, unopened box of M&M peanut candy. She took twenty bottles and the box of M&Ms up to her room, then eating one pack for energy, she went back out into the heat with a half-drunk bottle of water in her hand.

She was going to see if that hardware store Matt had mentioned had a portable generator, one small enough that she could haul it up to her room. She might as well try to make her Portland home as much a home as possible.

Otherwise, tonight she was going to be reading by candle and flashlight, and eating a cold dinner. Not to mention the fact that without a generator, a hot bath in that fantastic tub was impossible.

TEN

MATT ALMOST JUMPED out of bed as his alarm clock went off beside his bed. In two years, he hadn't ever had a need to use that stupid alarm clock. But today, he had a date, and he had a lot of cleaning and cooking to do before then.

He took a quick shower, then headed out into the kitchen. Buddy, his gray-haired old cat, looked up at him from the couch, yawned, and then went back to sleep.

"Too early, huh big fella?"

Buddy didn't even move. Matt couldn't blame him. It was early. Really early. The sun was barely coming up over Mt. Hood and the light that filled the penthouse apartment was orange-tinted. A low mist hung along the river and, as always, nothing seemed to be moving anywhere in the city.

He checked his security room, just to be sure he hadn't slept through any alarm.

Nothing.

Yesterday, Carey had made a couple of trips out of the hotel while he was over getting the chicken and eggs. He had recorded her dragging a pretty heavy-looking small generator back from the hardware store and in through the front door of the hotel on a hand truck. He hoped she had decided on a lower floor room, because he knew how much those little machines weighed and he couldn't imagine her dragging it up more than a few flights of stairs.

A couple hours later, just before sundown, she had made a few more trips to nearby stores, clearly for electrical supplies on one trip, food supplies on another.

After the sun had gone down, it was clear she hadn't picked a lower floor. She was on the top floor and that impressed him. No wonder she had survived for the past three years. She was one tough woman.

Lights, for the first time in two years, were coming from another building in the city below him. She had picked a room facing out over the river, away from his building, but he could still see her lights.

All evening, his gaze kept going to the lights. He so much wanted to know what she was doing, what she was thinking, find out more about her. The excitement and worry about the lunch tomorrow made reading almost impossible. Finally, he settled on a movie and didn't notice when she finally turned off her lights somewhere around midnight.

He couldn't believe she was there, that there was another sane person living in the city. At least, he hoped she was sane.

The first thing he needed to do this morning was bread the chicken, get it ready. Then he planned on going over to Powells and do some cleaning. After that, he would take a shower and do the cooking.

As the chicken fried, he would bake rolls and do the deviled eggs. The last thing he would do before leaving was pick some ears of corn and boil them.

The brown wicker picnic basket sat on the breakfast table, ready to be filled, a constant reminder of the hoped-for lunch ahead.

He made himself some quick breakfast, then breaded the chicken, then with cleaning supplies in his backpack, a rifle in one hand and a long-handled squeegee in the other, he headed out to Powells Bookstore.

The morning was cool, the city deathly silent, the streets still in shadow. He figured the best time to do the cleaning he wanted to do in their picnic area was before it got hot. That way, he could also go home and take a shower before cooking.

The area outside the rare book room on the top floor of Powells luckily didn't have many skeletons in it. He used an empty book cart and a blanket to gather the few there were and move them into another room. Then he wiped down one of the big, old wooden tables right in front of the window in the corner. He used the long-handled squeegee to wash the tall windows, and a push broom to move most of the dust out of the area on the hardwood floor.

He stood back and stared at the area. He had loved bookstores before the disaster, had raided a lot of them since. He had more books than he wanted to even count now. This felt like the perfect place for a picnic, and she had suggested it. Did that mean she loved books as much as he did? He hoped so.

He took out a checkered tablecloth he had found in the same store as the picnic basket and spread it on the table. If she got here before he did, she would know he had been here and got the space ready, and that he was coming back.

The sun was just starting to break down into the

streets as he finished the last sweeping. He had cleaned them a perfect place to have a picnic and get to know each other.

He hoped the lunch went as well as the place she had picked.

He could feel himself starting to get nervous. He was going to be lucky to get out a word at first. Figuring out what to talk about had always been his problem on dates. He had no doubt that he and Carey had more than enough to talk about, considering what they had both been through over the last three years. He just hoped he wouldn't have to start the conversation.

He glanced at his watch. He needed to get going. He wanted to have more than enough time to get home, take a shower, fry chicken, make the other things, and get back here right on time for his first date in over three years.

He had a date. That was something he never thought he would ever have again.

A date.

He whistled all the way back to his building.

ELEVEN

FOR CAREY, the morning before her first post-disaster date seemed to drag.

She had woken up at the first light streaming in through her east-facing windows. The bed had been comfortable, the room great. She had opened a few windows just before going to bed to get the cool evening breeze. Now it felt almost cold, a feeling she loved and had missed since leaving the coast. She'd leave those windows open until the day started to heat up, then close them and the drapes to keep the room cool for later this evening.

She checked her watch. Six in the morning.

Six hours until lunch.

Six hours with nothing to do but shower, get dressed, and walk the fifteen or so blocks up to Powells Bookstore on Burnside. If she stated now, she'd be about five hours early. Maybe she could go a little early and do some cleaning, get the space ready for a picnic.

She liked that idea.

She liked having something to do in her day, something to look forward to. Many mornings over the last three years, she had woken up with no idea what to do for the day. Especially that first year. Many days that year, she had just stayed in bed, cuddling with her cats, only getting up for food and the bathroom. Sometimes she just read, taking her mind away into a made-up world, other times she just slept and lay there, staring at the ceiling.

More than likely, a doctor would have called her depressed. And damn it, she had a right to be depressed. The world had ended, everyone had died, leaving her alone. That would depress a fence post.

During the second year, she had had less and less of those days in bed. This last year, not a one. Just surviving, keeping her home running and food on her table, kept her busy. There seemed to always be something to do, something to fix, some reason to get out of bed.

Today, she had a date.

She lay there, thinking of Matt's wonderful face, his deep voice, his alluring smile. She sure hoped that what she saw was what she got with him.

"Okay, lazy, get up and get going."

Those words often got her out of bed. This morning was no exception. She took a quick, and very cold shower. Cold showers in the morning were a completely different animal than cold showers after a hot, sweaty day of walking. Cold, early-morning showers were just downright painful.

She finished dressing, then decided that the best thing to do was finish setting up her generator in the right place and then, if she had time, set up her kitchen. A decent set of goals for one morning.

The small generator she had managed to bang and lug up the stairs would run a small microwave and some lights at the same time. Last night, she had set up the generator two rooms down the hall, with it venting out an open window. That way, the sound of the motor running didn't bother her and she could still hear if someone was coming.

She had run electrical cords into a dozen rooms from that room, all dead lines. She actually didn't have a cord running through the door of her room. Instead, she had banged a small hole in the wall between her suite and the next and ran the cord through there. It never hurt to be safe, as Matt had said, especially in a big city.

If she did end up making this a regular home that she visited at times, and if she and Matt got alone, she might ask him for help in setting up a security system in the hotel at some point in the future. A lot of ifs there, though.

She went down to the suite with the generator, took the hand truck, and moved the generator out into the hall again. Five rooms down from her room, she found a new home for the generator and again got it vented out the window. Then, using a hammer she had gotten from the hardware store, she banged a small hole in the wall through to the next suite, hiding the hole with a chair.

Thirty minutes later, after a lot of banging out old plaster, she had managed to string an electrical cord through the suites, hiding the cord behind furniture and drapes in each suite. Then she picked up all the decoy cords out of the hallway and other rooms. Now, she felt even safer if someone came looking for her. They would have to trace a cord through five different suites to find hers.

Next, she took a bottle of water and headed down to a kitchen store she had seen yesterday. An hour and two trips later, she had a fully-stocked kitchen, with pans, plates, silverware, serving dishes. If she stayed long enough to store any kind of food, she'd have to connect the small fridge as well, but she didn't plan on staying in the city long enough for that.

Ten o'clock. Two hours until lunch. She had accomplished both of her goals and she still had two hours. She might die of impatience before this date happened.

She went back and took another, slightly longer, cold shower to get the dirt and sweat off her, then put on her last change of clean clothes. She was going to have to do some laundry later today. The bathtub was going to come in handy for more than just taking baths.

Or maybe she could just stop into a store and find some new clothes. After lunch, she just might do that. She had never been much of a shopper, mostly because of the money side of things. Now, it didn't matter. She had even used money one night during the first year to start a fire, just to show herself it didn't matter any more. Didn't help. She still hated shopping.

At eleven, she was ready to leave. She planned on stopping along the way, getting a few cleaning supplies, and getting to Powells a little early to clean up an area for her and Matt to eat in. It was the least she could do, considering he was bringing the fried chicken and who knew what else.

She moved to the window to shut out the warming air so that the suite would stay cool. But just before she pulled the old window down, she noticed a rumbling sound echoing over the silent city. She leaned out the window, trying to figure out where the rumbling was coming from.

She couldn't tell.

The sound seemed to echo off buildings, one second coming from the south, the next from the north. And it was still very faint.

She stayed at the window, watching for any sign of

movement, as the rumbling got slowly louder, seeming to fill every dead street with low thunder.

What could be causing such a sound?

A tank? A large truck pushing wrecks aside? Something massive, clearly, although she had no idea how sounds carried in an empty city.

Then she caught a glimpse of something moving across the river, way down the I-84 freeway toward the old airport.

She grabbed her binoculars. At first, she couldn't see anything. Then finally, she understood what had caused the sound, and what she saw sent chills down her spine.

Bikers.

A fairly large group of motorcycle riders were working their way slowly toward town, weaving in and around the wrecks, coming in on I-84 from the east. From the distance, she couldn't tell how many, but more than she wanted to be around, that was for sure.

Her best friend had been raped by two members of a motorcycle club back in high school.

She hated motorcycles.

She hated bikers.

Suddenly, date or no date, the city didn't seem to be the place she wanted to be anymore.

TWELVE

AFTER MATT GOT BACK to his apartment from cleaning up the area in Powells, he saw that Carey had come out of her hotel twice, both for different types of supplies.

Just seeing her working on a place to stay in town excited him. She was as good-looking as he remembered from yesterday. And certainly focused.

He watched her for a moment, then went back to the kitchen and fried the chicken, at the same time baking some rolls. He had just taken the chicken out, and the rolls, and was finishing up the deviled eggs when his alarm went off.

Was Carey leaving already for Powells? He glanced at his watch. It was quarter to eleven.

He left the eggs and moved to the security room, expecting to see a red light on the area outside of Carey's building. But instead, the light was blinking way out on Interstate 84.

He dropped into his chair and flicked up the camera for that area. What he saw rocked him back.

Bikers.

A lot of bikers.

A string of at least two dozen men, and a few women, all on large motorcycles, were working their way slowly through the car wrecks that littered the freeway. A couple of the bikes were pulling small trailers, and every one of the people were dressed in black leather.

Matt hadn't much cared one way or another for the biker groups back when he was in school. He knew that most of them were made up of regular people, folks who just liked riding motorcycles. Some of the main motorcycle clubs were just doctors and lawyers who could afford the pricey Harley Davidson bikes, plus a few mechanics and others who had had the same bike for years and kept it up. In fact, his best friend in college, Danny, had a Harley his dad had bought him. Danny put on his leathers and went for a ride every time he got the chance. Matt had even gone with him a few times, but just never caught the excitement that Danny felt about the experience.

Now, here was a biker group, or at least a group of people traveling together on motorcycles. More than likely, that was the case. And considering all the wrecks along the roads that blocked traffic almost everywhere, using a motorcycle seemed logical. He would have made the same choice if he had decided to go exploring in other cities, and had, at one point last year, even scouted out a few of the motorcycle dealerships in the downtown area, looking for the right equipment.

Matt watched the bikers work their way slowly around a wreck of about fifteen piled-up cars, not seeming to be in any hurry. He took a deep breath and tried to count them, and really look at the faces as they passed a camera he had secured inside a building near the freeway.

Most of them looked dirty, but that could be just from riding. All of them carried rifles within easy reach on their bikes, and a few had pistols stuck in their belts. Twenty-three of them, all but four men.

Suddenly, he remembered Carey.

And their date.

He flicked the monitor back to the camera showing the area around the Embassy Suites entrance. Carey must still be inside, otherwise one of his motion sensors would have activated again. She had no idea what was riding at her.

"Get a grip on yourself," Matt said aloud, letting his voice calm himself down. "These guys are more than likely friendly."

Or maybe they weren't, but until he knew for sure, it was going to be a lot safer for him, and for Carey, to not let the gang know they were here.

He flipped the monitor back to the motorcycle riders. At the speed they were traveling, and the amount of blockage they faced ahead, they wouldn't be into the main part of town for at least another half hour, more than likely an hour.

Maybe they were just heading through, going toward California to spend the winter in the sun, and wouldn't even stop. It was still early in the day. That was possible, but again, he didn't dare take the chance.

And he didn't want Carey to take the chance either. This might be the friendliest bunch of humans he had ever met, but with that many of them, he wanted to be damn sure before he strode up to the front of that line of bikes.

He punched another button and a few moments later a picture of the bikers came out of his printer. It showed at least fifteen of them. He folded it and stuffed it in his pocket.

Then with one more check to make sure Carey had not left the old hotel just yet, he sprinted for the door. On the way, he grabbed a couple of deviled eggs to stop his rumbling stomach, his rifle, and his shoulder belt with ammunition. Then he grabbed his pistol, made sure it was loaded, and stuck it inside his belt behind his back. In three years he had hoped to find more people. Now, suddenly, in just two days, he had gotten his wish.

Just not the way he had expected.

THIRTEEN

CAREY STOOD, almost frozen in the window, watching the pack of motorcycle riders work their way toward her.

"Get a grip, girl," she said. "You got to get out of here."

She quickly tossed all her clothing in her pack, her food, her flashlight and other tools, then made sure the pistol was loaded and ready and stuffed it in her belt.

She did the same for the rifle and slung it over her shoulder. Then she went back to the window. The rumbling seemed to fill everything around her, even though the bikers were clearly miles away. More than likely, when the city had all its people, you never would have heard the bikers from this distance. But now, there just wasn't any other sound on the clear summer day.

Suddenly, from the hallway, Matt's voice shouted out.

"Carey? You still up here?"

She couldn't decide if she should say anything or not.

"Carey? If you're still here, let me know which room. It's me, Matt. You remember, your lunch date? I'd never normally come up here, but there's something happening I think you should know about."

He had come to warn her. That made her smile, even with the rumbling filling the room from the window.

"Open your window and listen if you don't believe me. I have a picture of what's coming up the freeway to show you."

He knew she would be careful, not trust him for barging in like this, so he had brought proof. The guy could think under pressure, that was for sure.

She opened the door, not bothering to take her rifle off her shoulder.

He was standing down the hallway, his back to a wall, his rifle also shouldered. But this time he was carrying one. He looked slightly winded and was sweating. More than likely, he had run from the Baxter building to warn her.

Her stomach twisted at seeing him again. He was better looking than she remembered from yesterday. It was stunning how attracted she was to this man.

"Bikers," she said. "I heard them and caught a few glimpses of them coming in on I-84. I hate bikers."

He nodded, coming toward her, offering her a picture.

She took it and stared. The focus was from the top of a pole along the freeway, and it showed at least ten, maybe more, motorcycle riders working their way past a large pile-up of cars. The picture made her shudder and she handed it back to him.

"What are you planning on doing?" she asked, again stunned at how much she was attracted to the man standing in front of her. She got no hint that he was dangerous. Her mother's voice came drifting back to her. *Trust your instincts with men.*

"Watch them," Matt said. "Just watch them, unless I become completely convinced they are not a problem. Then I wouldn't mind talking to them, but not until I'm convinced they are not dangerous."

"You're not planning on walking up to them, unarmed, with your hands in the air, are you?" she asked.

"Did you look at that picture?" he asked back, his face slightly red.

She smiled at him. "A joke."

It took him a moment, then he relaxed and smiled, his face going to a little darker shade of red. She liked that a lot. A man who could blush. How great was that?

"So what would you suggest I do?" she asked.

He pointed at the shuffled footprints in the hallway. "If they're the type to go looking for people, they'd find you here easily. And worst case, if they are the type to go looking, I don't think you're going to want to be found."

"I agree," she said. "Have I ever told you I hate bikers."

He smiled. "Yeah, think I heard that before."

"Good," she said. "Just wanted you to know."

"I've got the Baxter building completely secured," Matt said. "And enough cameras around the outside of the city to watch these people's movements until we get to know them better."

She stared at him, then glanced down at the image of the bikers working their way along the freeway. She could hear their bikes through the window she had left open in the room behind her, the sounds echoing like thunder on a clear day. She didn't trust Matt completely by a long ways, but she had a hunch he was prepared for something like this.

She could go with him, or she could just head away from the gang, over the hills to the west and back to the beach. But that wouldn't solve the problem she had come here to solve. And the thought of leaving Matt without getting to know him twisted her stomach more than going with him did.

But she also knew he was right. She couldn't stay here in this room. Okay, so choose. She didn't want to head home yet. So going with him, for the moment, seemed to be the best of a bunch of bad choices.

"So, the offer of breakfast didn't work to get me to go back to your place," she said, "so now you bring on a biker gang. Original, I must say."

He looked at her, puzzled for a moment, then she smiled at him again. "Another joke. Lighten up, will you?"

He laughed. "Just not used to anyone's jokes but mine."

"Yeah, I know that feeling."

"I've got most of lunch cooked, if my cat hasn't eaten it all by the time we get back. We can just move the picnic from Powells to my place. From there, we can watch what these visitors are going to do through my security system."

"You have a cat?"

"I'm owned by a cat," Matt said, smiling that wonderful smile of his at her. "He lets me live with him."

"I have two and I miss them a lot right now."

"Cat fix and a fried chicken picnic. That's the best offer I can make."

The sounds of the motorcycles got even louder over the city, almost echoing in the hallway. The idea of facing a motorcycle gang scared her beyond words. But at the same time, she didn't want to just run. She wanted to get to know this man standing across from her. Staying to get to know him might very well risk her life, but as Matt had decided yesterday, coming to her unarmed, sometimes the risks were worth the payoff.

"Best offer I've had in three years. I'll take it."

His face lit up. "Great."

Together, they checked her suite to make sure she hadn't forgotten anything before heading out into the street. For some reason, she had a feeling, she wasn't coming back.

FOURTEEN

MATT LED THE WAY through the wrecks and debris
that covered the sidewalks and streets toward the Baxter
building. The sound of the motorcycles echoed through
the tall buildings like a dangerous storm, sometimes
louder, sometimes only distant, but clearly coming.

Matt was very relieved that Carey had agreed to
come back with him. At the same time, he was worried.
He didn't really know this woman, yet he was inviting
her up into his apartment, and along the way, just from
sheer necessity, he was going to show her some of his
security measures. Not very smart on his part, if she
turned out to be a dangerous problem.

Nothing he seemed to be doing around this woman
was very smart when looked at from a position of survival. Yet, there was something about Carey that made
him want to trust her. He just hoped that instinct was
coming from his gut instead of the desire to have companionship after three years. He had learned, early in
school, that sometimes his brain migrated to a position a
distance below his belt, and when down there made
very bad decisions, especially concerning women.

Actually, decisions made below his belt were *always* about women. This didn't feel like one of those decisions. This felt like Carey could be a friend, like Betty the cheerleader had been. Of course, he wanted more than just friendship, but that would come later, after a lot of trust was built.

But right now, those bikers coming in on Interstate 84 made any slow and easy progress getting to trust Carey impossible. He was going to have to trust her now, if he wanted to help her stay out of the way of that group. And since he wanted to spend more time with her, and didn't want her chased out of town, or even worse, killed, then he was going to have to take some chances.

And on the other side, he knew she was taking some large chances as well with him, chances she probably shouldn't be taking. Clearly the picture and the sounds of those motorcycles had spooked her. Enough that she thought he was the better of two bad options at the moment.

At least she was making jokes about it. She had gotten him a few times already. It was going to take some time to get used to her sense of humor.

He got to the main door of the Baxter building and glanced back at her.

She paused, looking up and down the street. "Aren't they going to be able to follow us in here as well? If they wanted to, that is."

He pointed to the sidewalk they had just walked along.

She nodded. "No footprints. Smart."

"I keep all the sidewalks in a two block radius of this door blown free of dust."

"That has to be a lot of fun," she said, smiling at him.

"If you call digging dirt out of your ears for days later fun. And also I sweep this lobby regularly, along with most of the other hotels in a few block radius. They might figure out someone's around here by the lack of dust, but they won't know exactly where."

She nodded. "Impressive. You've given this a lot of thought and a lot of work."

"I read a lot of science fiction as a kid," Matt said, remembering the large bookshelf in his bedroom when he was in high school. "And I'm more afraid of the human animal than any other. Especially in situations we find ourselves in now."

She nodded at that statement as well, so he went on.

"Besides, before all this, my job was with a security company. After two years with them, this kind of paranoid thinking sort of got in my blood."

"And that's supposed to encourage me?" she asked, smiling at him.

"Sometimes paranoid is beautiful," he said, trying to make a lame joke in return. "Wait until you see the rest of my paranoid delusions."

"I'm looking forward to it," she said.

He headed in through the big glass doors to the lobby of the Baxter building. The lobby had a marble-like floor, with a number of skeletons of people scattered around the large area, including two security guards behind the desk. He had started to clear out the bodies in the lobby one day, then realized that if he did that, he would be leading someone right to him. He hadn't noticed the bodies in a year, but now, with Carey with him, he was seeing everything, as if he was looking through her eyes.

The bodies in the rest of the building he had moved out, laying them all together in a large meeting room in City Hall. It was the best he could do for them, and that task alone had taken him almost two weeks.

She had followed him inside the lobby and was scanning the large area as they walked, their steps echoing in the high-ceilinged space.

"Stairwell doors are locked and bolted," he said, pointing to the staircase he sometimes used. "And I can block the entrances at the top as well so it would take a tank to get through. I also locked all the other stairwell doors in the buildings around this one. Same reason as blowing off the dust."

She nodded and said nothing.

He took a key out of his pocket and inserted it into a slot beside the third elevator call button. Then he touched the button. The elevator door slid open without the customary chime.

He stepped back and smiled at her. "Going up?"

She looked shocked. "You have enough electricity to run an elevator?"

"I do," he said, proud of the accomplishment of hooking up one elevator to an electrical circuit off a series of generators in a maintenance building on the roof. It had been a difficult job, especially triggering extra generators to start when he touched the call button on any floor.

She stared at the open elevator. For a moment, he didn't think she was going to get in, so he stepped inside, holding the door open for her just like he used to do for people in the days before the disaster.

She stared into his eyes for a long few seconds. He could see worry about trusting him, and also intelligence in her eyes as he stared back. She had studied him, just as he had studied her. She didn't like taking this much risk, and neither did he, but for the moment they both needed to.

And clearly, she was as attracted to him as he was to her. He didn't know if that was a good thing or not, but it felt right.

Finally, she nodded and joined him on the elevator.

"Sorry we couldn't have got to know each other a little slower," he said as the door closed and they rode upward in a strained silence for a moment. "I was really looking forward to our picnic."

"So was I," she said.

"I figured you would want to get out of the way of the biker group if you could, and this is the best, and safest place, since you don't have a home and security of your own set up here yet."

"I appreciate the thought," she said. "And if this group turns out to be a nasty bunch, I'm going to be really happy you helped me stay out of their way."

She sighed, then went on. "Actually, when you showed up, I was about ready to run over the west hills and get away from here. I'm glad you talked me into staying."

"So am I," he said as the elevator slowed and the door opened onto his penthouse apartment. "I can't eat all this fried chicken by myself."

She laughed as he stepped out of the elevator ahead of her, dropped his two guns into the rack beside the door, and headed past the kitchen counter toward the security room.

"Make yourself at home," he said. "Water and other drinks in the fridge. Bathroom is off to the right. I'm going to see where our friendly bike riders are. Then I'll work at finishing our picnic lunch."

He didn't even look back. He figured the best way to get her comfortable with his place, and with him, was to take the chance and let her just look around on her own.

He had taken this many chances so far. He just hoped one more wouldn't kill him.

FIFTEEN

CAREY STEPPED OFF the elevator and stood in silence as Matt dropped his guns on a rack and headed for his security room. She couldn't believe that she was actually in a penthouse apartment with a man she had only met the day before. How stupid was she becoming? She was going to have to sit down and have a good talk with herself when this was over, if she survived it.

And when she got back to the coast, she was going to have to think a lot more about security. The picture of those bikers coming down the freeway had scared her more than she wanted to admit.

Sure, she knew that most people who rode motorcycles were just regular people, and the ones that went on those "runs" were no different. Even most of the motorcycle clubs were just lawyers and doctors and corporate business people having a good time on their weekends.

And she knew it was logical, with the condition of the roads, for people to travel these days on motorcycles. But the image of Diana, one of her best friends in high school, laying in that hospital, beaten unconscious and raped by two bikers from San Francisco, had haunted Carey for years. Anytime she saw anyone in leathers, she stayed away. Didn't matter who or what they were.

She pushed the image of Diana back and looked around at the bright, sun-lit apartment beyond the foyer area.

Matt had left himself clearly unarmed. Again, he was trusting her blindly.

She watched him disappear into the open doorway as the elevator door slid closed behind her. She glanced back at it and then, without thinking, reached over and touched the call button.

The door slid open without a problem, the empty inside of the elevator inviting her to step back in.

She stared at the open elevator for a moment, thinking maybe she should just go down to the street. From there, she could somehow manage to hike out of town and up into the west hills where she doubted anyone on a motorcycle could find her, even if they knew she existed.

But for some reason this man trusted her. Not only to approach her yesterday unarmed, but to leave her alone like this in his apartment. He was doing everything he could to ease her worries, including not locking her in here.

She shook her head. She had come to the city to find other people, see who else was alive. Now she was doing that, and she wanted to run away. How crazy was that?

"Crazy," she said softly.

She had to admit, having Matt come for her today when he discovered the bikers made her feel good. She felt lucky to have met him, actually. Maybe she could get *really* lucky and get to know him even better.

She pushed that thought away, then repeated to herself softly, "Go slowly. Go slowly."

She let the elevator door close again. It seemed she was staying.

She slipped off her backpack and leaned it against the wall beside Matt's gun rack. He had three nice rifles, one was a twenty-two about the size of hers, one clearly was a deer rifle, and a third with a scope that looked like a sniper rifle more than a hunting rifle. From this height, that sniper rifle could do a lot of damage. She wondered how good a shot he was with it. Maybe someday, she'd ask him.

He also had left the pistol he had been carrying, but she didn't recognize its size and brand at all.

She stood her rifle up beside her pack, keeping her pistol in her belt where she could grab it quickly if she needed to. She was taking enough chances, no point in taking any more than she had to.

A large archway in front of her led out of the foyer area and into the apartment. She moved inside, slowly, looking around as she went. High windows and sky-lights made the entire space seem as if it were as much outdoors as inside. It also smelled of fried chicken like her mom used to make, and fresh bread, something she knew well from her own bread-making at home.

Then something dawned on her.

The apartment was cool.

Oh, my, god, he had air-conditioning. The room was comfortable, actually, even with the sun beating in through the tall windows.

Matt had air-conditioning running. She was almost in love with him now. Any man who could get air-conditioning running on a hot summer's day deserved her respect. She could feel the cool draft swirling on her bare arms. This guy really was good at mechanical things.

She had a hunch, that wasn't all he was good at.

She pushed that thought back hard, then paused and listened for a moment. She couldn't even hear the generators running. He had said they were on the roof. They must be in a silenced room or something.

Power to run a full kitchen, lights, computers, air-conditioning, and elevators. His generator set-up must really be something very powerful.

The apartment had an organized feel to it. And it was clean, very clean. Just standing in the entrance made her realize how dirty and sweat-covered she was, just from the walk across town.

A large kitchen area filled the middle of the space to the left, with hanging pots and just about every imaginable appliance on the counter tops and shelves. Clearly Matt liked to cook, and seemed to know what he was doing, from the looks of the set-up of the kitchen.

A large bowl of fried chicken sat half covered on one side of the counter, and a wicker basket filled another corner of the table. She smiled at that. He had found a picnic basket. He really was one for details.

She walked through the kitchen, touching the countertop, noting where things were. She could cook in this place, that was for sure. It was set up as a chef's kitchen. And right now, she was very hungry. She hadn't really had that much breakfast this morning, originally thinking that she would save herself for the fried chicken. She glanced at her watch. It still wasn't noon, but even still, she was going to need something soon.

A plate of deviled eggs sat near the picnic basket. She couldn't help herself. She took one and the wonderful mustard and egg flavor melted in her mouth. They were the best she had ever tasted, even better than her mother's. If these eggs were any sign of how good a cook he was, she might actually gain weight hanging around here.

She took another egg and the complaints from her stomach eased.

It looked like he had gotten interrupted by the bikers right at the moment he was about to start cooking some ears of corn. His garden must be really good. She couldn't get corn to grow in her garden on the coast. Too damp, wrong climate.

A pile of books sat against the window, and one entire interior wall of the large apartment was covered in books.

There was a couch and a large, overstuffed recliner in front of a giant screen television. And another matching chair in front of a window facing Mt. Hood. Two books were on the floor beside that chair, and another on a small end table. Clearly Matt liked to read. Maybe as much as she did. That was good.

She had almost exactly the same television set-up at home, same big screen and all. The only difference was that instead of one of her cats sleeping on the couch, Matt had a big, older-looking gray cat who was now staring at her, its tail twitching.

"Who are you?" she asked the cat.

The cat's ears went back slightly, and again its tail twitched, as if it were about to bolt. She decided to give the cat some room, so she turned toward a deck area on the other side of a large, sliding glass door. It looked inviting, but hot, so she just stared at it for a moment without going outside, then turned to study the apartment some more.

Off to the right were some private rooms, more than likely his bedroom and the bathroom he had indicated.

She was going to have to use it shortly, and wash her face as well.

She stared at the big, gray cat as it stared back at her. She missed her cats more than she wanted to admit. She just hoped they were still there waiting for her when she got back.

"Okay, I won't try to pet you yet," she said to the big cat on the couch. With one last look at the public area of the beautiful apartment, she took two more deviled eggs, one for her, one for Matt, and headed toward the room he had vanished into.

What she found there surprised her even more. Inside what once must have been a large study with one wall of glass was an entire room of computers, recording devices, and monitors. On one interior wall was a map of the entire Portland area, with blinking red lights in different places.

Matt was in a large, high-backed chair, staring at a big screen.

"What are they doing?" she asked.

He started, as if he had forgotten she was even there, then without turning around pointed at the screen. "They are just getting to the I-5 junction."

"These are heavenly," she said, passing Matt one of the eggs, then taking a bite out of the other one.

"Thanks," he said, putting the entire egg in his mouth. "Old family recipe."

She turned and stared out the window. From this height, she could see the opposite side of the river where I-84 ended into I-5. Coming in on I-84 you had to either pick north or south on I-5. The city of Portland was a beautiful sight from that intersection, its tall buildings tucked along the river and against the hills beyond.

"Are these windows reflective?" she asked as she saw something move.

"Perfectly," he said. "But when the sun starts going down, if they are still around, we're going to have to go dark in the main areas." He pointed to the top of the big window. "No drapes."

"Never needed them before, I bet."

"Whoever owned this place didn't seem to think they needed them back when there were people around." He went back to watching the bikers on the screen.

From what she could tell from the images on the screen, he had a camera on something high, directly in the middle of the intersection. There were a couple of car wrecks clogging both directions, but not enough to stop a motorcycle from getting past. She had to admit it made sense to travel on motorcycles. She had considered one for the trip over here, but just couldn't come to make herself learn how to ride one without help.

The bikers looked dirty, which meant nothing in the current world of ruin. It was almost impossible to avoid the dust and dirt that covered everything. She was covered in it as well, and more than likely looked almost as dirty, and that was just from a fast walk across town.

Most of the men had long beards, many of them had their hair pulled back in pony tails. All of them had rifles in their saddlebags and a few carried pistols on their hips.

She could see a few women as well on bikes, which encouraged her. Maybe this was just a group exploring, looking for more survivors, and it was just her old thinking of biker gangs being dangerous that had spooked her. But even if they were friendly, it was a heck of a lot better to be safe and find out first what they were doing.

Matt had been right. This apartment with all his security precautions, felt very, very safe.

And cool. She hadn't needed air-conditioning on the coast. She didn't know how much she missed it here.

"Twenty-three of them," Matt said, nodding as the last one passed under his camera. He tapped his keyboard and the image on the big screen switched to showing the bikers slowly moving south on I-5.

She watched Matt stare at the screen for a moment, admiring his strong shoulders and brown hair. She just hoped this guy was as safe as she felt he was. There was nothing in his apartment that looked odd besides this room. Nothing felt dangerous, nothing set off her warning bells, and that worried her too. No man was perfect. Not even Paine.

"This room is really something," she said. "I'm impressed."

Matt smiled up at her. "Free supplies, lots of spare time, knowledge of electronics, and enough paranoia to fill a small lake will get you a room like this."

"Makes sense."

"Thanks."

"You think those guys saw your lights last night? Or mine?" She didn't tell him that she had gone up to the roof of her building at one point and just stared up at his lights coming from this place. He was right, his place did look like a beacon from a distance.

Matt shrugged. "I doubt it. If they came all the way in on I-84 from the east, then more than likely they camped last night up at Multnomah Falls in the Columbia Gorge. There's food in the lodge there, enough beds for a group this size, and good drinking water. And that would put them in here just about this time, if they started early."

"Makes sense," she said. "I hope you're right."

"So do I," he said.

He glanced around. Suddenly, he must have realized she was standing and he was sitting. He jumped up. "Let me get you a chair."

She held her hand up. "I'll get it. You keep watching."

He smiled at her and nodded. "Kitchen table has a few chairs. Usually I take one and Buddy takes the other."

"Buddy's the cat's name?"

"Yeah, took me six months to get him to trust me," Matt said, dropping back into the big chair. "There were still a few roving packs of feral cats in the city when I came back two years ago. They've all mostly disappeared now. No food. I bet you really miss your cats. I'd miss Buddy if I had to leave him for any time."

"Yeah, I now understand that feeling."

She went back out into the living area of the big apartment and toward the dining table, stopping near the cat. "Well, Buddy, are you going to let me pet you?"

"Careful," Matt called out from the room behind her. "He's got claws."

She laughed. Both her cats had claws that she tried to keep trimmed just enough to keep the points from becoming razor-sharp, but not enough to make the cats defenseless.

Buddy sort of stared at her, clearly not sure what to do. She eased out her hand and he leaned forward and sniffed it. Then he turned his head indicating that she should scratch his ears.

She did as the cat instructed, taking her time and

giving his ears a good rubbing. When she finally stopped, Buddy looked up at her and then stood, purring.

"You're just a big softy," she said, scratching his back and then his ears again.

"Now that's something I wouldn't have believed possible," Matt said from the doorway.

Buddy heard his voice and jumped down from the couch, walking toward Matt as if what had just happened went on every day.

"I'm a cat person," she said, smiling at Matt's stunned look before she turned to get the chair. She didn't want to tell him how much simply petting Buddy had done to make her feel better.

By the time she got the chair back into the computer room, along with the plate of deviled eggs, Matt was again in front of the big screen, watching the bikers move south on I-5, heading for the bridge over the river.

Buddy was on his lap, purring as Matt petted him with one hand.

There was just something about that scene that made her relax just a little more. Sitting there, petting a cat and staring at a monitor seemed so normal for him.

And right now, she really missed normal, needed normal, wanted normal more than anything else she had ever desired.

She sat there, staring at Matt and Buddy as outside, the gang of bikers worked their way closer.

SIXTEEN

"DAMN IT," Matt said, staring at the big screen in his security room. "They're coming into town."

Carey felt her stomach twist into a knot. She was sitting beside, and slightly behind, Matt, with a clear view of the monitor. She watched as the lead two motorcycles, without even a second of hesitation, left I-5 on the I-405 ramp. The two moved slowly around a large pile-up of cars, then accelerated through a clear stretch of highway.

Blinking red lights on Matt's big board started to flash as the two lead bikers went quickly through two of his motion detector areas. Matt had to jump two cameras ahead to get to a view that allowed him to see the lead bikers on the monitor.

Carey watched, stunned at seeing this many other people alive, and this close, as the motorcycles passed the exit to Beaverton that would have taken them away from the city. They got off at the Chambers Street exit, working their way slowly past a pile-up at the top.

"They seem to all know exactly where they are going," Matt said, shaking his head as he switched the monitor back to the interchange, then to a camera along the way, then back to the two lead bikes.

"It sure looks that way," Carey said.

"The group is spread out for a mile. They must have the night's camp sight planned out ahead. That kind of planning would make sense, considering how many of them there are."

"They are also in contact with each other," Carey said, pointing at the screen. "See the headsets with the microphones?"

"You're right," Matt said. "At least one in every small bunch has one on. This is a very organized group."

Carey wasn't sure if that was a good thing, or a bad thing. After being so alone for three years, it was surprising how dangerous other people felt to her.

Her mother's voice echoed again in her head. *Such a brave little girl.* Carey ignored it. There was a difference between being brave and being stupid, sometimes a fine line difference, but still a difference. And being worried about these new arrivals, maybe even afraid of them, wasn't a bad thing.

"How many cameras do you have in the city itself?" Carey asked.

"Not that many, actually," Matt said. "Most everything I have is on the main ways in. I planned to put up more, but after the first year, there didn't seem to be much of a priority. And I had to go over to one of the stores in Beaverton to get more equipment." He shrugged and smiled at her. "Never really got around to it."

"I'm amazed you have this many," she said. "You climbed a lot of light poles."

He laughed. "It's easy, once you have the right

equipment and get the hang of it. I was trained for it in the security job."

Carey couldn't imagine climbing a pole like that, especially with the knowledge that if she fell, there would be no one to help her, no hospital to go to, no ambulance to take her. Over the last three years, thoughts like that had kept her out of many dangerous situations.

The two lead bikers were out of any camera range. Carey wasn't sure why having them in the city worried her so much. She just kept repeating to herself that bikers were just normal people who ride motorcycles. And if you had to travel in this age of clogged roads, bikes were the best way. In fact, maybe the only way to go any real distance. But still, the fact that there were so many of them scared her.

Carey looked at the big board of lights on the city map. "Are we going to know when they get near this building?"

"We will," Matt said, smiling at her. "I have at least two dozen cameras around this building covering the streets in all directions for five blocks."

"Let's just hope they're nice people," Carey said.

"More than likely they are," Matt said, pointing at the screen showing a group of five getting off the freeway on the Chambers Street exit. "The license plates on most of those bikes are Nevada. A couple are Arizona, and I think I saw one Utah plate."

"Nevada makes sense," she said, nodding, thinking about the military establishments there. "A lot of people in Nevada might have survived."

Matt turned slowly to look at her. "How do you know that? You said yesterday that you knew what caused all this. How? And what was it?"

She laughed. "Just like you and all the security stuff,

I had a past as well. Tell you what, after we find out where the group out there is going, I'll tell you over that picnic you offered me."

He looked at her, then smiled. "Deal."

She could have just sat there and stared into his eyes for the next ten minutes, but instead she said, "Would you mind if I use your bathroom to get cleaned up?"

"Not at all. It's down the hallway on the left, extra clean towels on the shelf in there. And be careful, the hot water in the shower is really hot."

"You have hot water? I haven't had a hot shower since I left the coast. I think I have found heaven."

He laughed again. "I don't know about heaven, but this place does have air-conditioning, hot water, and a washer and dryer if you want to wash a few clothes. They're just off the bathroom."

She again looked into his eyes. "Thank you, Matt, for the hospitality, and the concern for my safety."

"You are welcome," he said. "It's going to be nice to have someone to talk to over lunch. Besides Buddy here, that is. It's been a long three years."

"For me too," she said.

With that, she got up and headed to get her back-pack. She would take him up on his offer to wash some clothes. Washing what she had at this point made more sense than going out looking for new clothes, considering that outside the building, the streets of Portland had people in it again.

SEVENTEEN

MATT WATCHED CAREY leave the room, then went back to scratching Buddy's ears and staring at the bikers as they moved through the wreck at the Chambers Street exit and went somewhere into downtown Portland. After ten more minutes, the last one went by and there was nothing left to see.

So far none of the bikers in the city had entered an area of town that he had motion sensors and cameras. So until they did, he was going to have to wait.

He set the loud alarm that had woken him up yesterday morning when Carey entered town. If any of the bikers went into an area where he had a camera and a motion sensor, the alarm would tell him.

He stood, easing Buddy to the floor. "Come on, old guy," Matt said to his cat. "Nothing more we can do here at the moment. We have a guest to finish cooking for." He picked up the plate full of the remaining deviled eggs, popped one into his mouth, and headed for the kitchen.

As he went through the living room, he could hear the faint sounds of the shower running. He couldn't believe that a beautiful woman was in his shower. Maybe he was still in bed and dreaming. Maybe the world really hadn't ended, and he hadn't spent the last three years alone.

Didn't he wish.

He stopped for a moment and listened. The shower sounds were real.

Carey really was in there.

And now he needed to fix her something to eat. Until she had mentioned the picnic, and brought him the deviled eggs he had made, he had been too busy to realize just how hungry he had become. It wasn't often he skipped meals, and his morning exercise routine. Of course, cleaning up the corner of Powells had been some decent exercise. Oh, well, maybe they could use that space another time, for another picnic.

Buddy followed him into the open kitchen area. "I missed your breakfast too, didn't I?"

Buddy banged against his leg and then walked over and sat down at his empty cat bowl.

"All right, you first," Matt said, laughing. He grabbed the half-used bag of cat food from the shelf and fed Buddy quickly.

Then he moved the chicken to the dining room table, along with the eggs and rolls, putting the picnic basket on the floor by the window.

Then he started a pot of water boiling for the corn, added a little butter-flavored powder and some salt to the water, then started to peel the ears of corn.

"That was wonderful," Carey said.

She came out of the hallway from the bathroom carrying her backpack in one hand. "Thank you. I hope you don't mind that I've taken you up on washing some clothes."

Her long brown hair was still damp and hanging

over her shoulders. Her face had a red glow to it, as if she had scrubbed it more than once. She had on the same blouse and jeans, and except for the pistol tucked in her belt, she looked more like a college student than a survivor who was still alive three years after the world had ended.

Matt took a deep breath and let it out slowly, trying to get his heart to calm down. She was better looking than he had even thought yesterday morning. Stunning was a better way of putting it.

She dropped her backpack near his gun rack, then took the pistol out of her belt and laid it on top of the pack. Clearly, she was starting to trust him a little more.

She turned and came back toward him. "You're sure on the washing? Water isn't an issue here?"

"No problem at all," he said. "I have filters keeping the water clean in the tank on the roof, and it's good to run more than I use every so often to help the process."

She laughed. "I wouldn't even have good water if I hadn't run a pipe down from a house above where I live. It had a natural well, and I somehow manage to keep the pump going and the long pipes not leaking too much."

Matt nodded. "Pumps can be a problem. I've had to replace two so far that pump water from the main gravity-fed lines under the street to the roof. Took me days to do each one."

"Amazing," she said, shaking her head. "Elevator, air-conditioning, water pumps. I could never keep a place like this going."

He smiled at her nice compliment, then held up an ear of fresh corn. "Corn on the cob with your fried chicken?"

Her face lit up like a kid's on Christmas morning.

"Oh, god, that sounds wonderful. What can I do to help?"

He glanced around at the kitchen he was used to being in alone, then pointed at the table. "Just sit there and tell me what you used to do before the world ended. And how you know what caused this mess."

"Sounds like I'm getting the better part of this deal," she said, laughing as she dropped into the chair he usually sat at. He was never going to get tired of her laugh. It had a high ring to it, and just made him want to smile.

"I don't think so," he said. "You know how many times I wished I had someone to talk to while I cooked."

"Actually, I do," she said, her smile fading slightly.

They held each other's gaze for a moment.

How dumb was he? Of course she knew what that was like. She had told him she had been alone the entire time as well. What was he thinking? He nodded and smiled. "Sorry."

She shrugged.

"To the story. I have cooking to do."

She laughed. "Ahh, where to start."

"The beginning," he said.

"Twenty-seven years ago I was born right here in Portland, grew up in Beaverton. My father was a stockbroker the entire time, my mother taught school."

As she was talking, he finished getting the corn ready and dropped it into the boiling water.

"My birthday's in October," he said. "I'll be twenty-seven then as well, also born right here, but grew up in Bend."

"May birthday for me," she said. "Looks like we're pretty close to the same age."

"So where did you go to college?" he asked, assuming that she had. He glanced at the table. Chicken, now cold, corn, eggs, rolls, what more did they need?

"Eugene," she said.

He stopped and stared at her. Eugene was the hometown of the University of Oregon. "You're kidding? So did I? What was your major?"

"Physics," she said. "I was working on my post-doctorate when all this happened. What was yours?"

No wonder he thought this woman was smart. She was. Anyone who could go that far in physics had to have a brain that was far beyond his.

He laughed. "Electrical engineering. No surprise, huh?" he said, indicating the room with all his equipment in it. "I got a four-year degree and came here to work. Best thing I could find was the alarm company. No regular engineering firm would hire me with only an undergrad degree and moderate grades."

"Turned out to be a great thing," she said, smiling at him.

"Guess it did, didn't it."

He looked up from the boiling corn and into her eyes again. "So how come we never ran into each other at the university? I think I would have remembered seeing you."

She shrugged. "Actually, probably not. I was the shy, bookworm type, stayed in the dorms for the first three years, mostly just studying. I was a freshman at seventeen and never really paid much attention to the party scene. Actually, I was living here three years ago, working on my post-doc in electromagnetics."

"Electromagnetics? What were you doing in Portland?"

"Working at a lab for a Dr. Canfield."

Now he was really impressed. Canfield was a

known name, not only in science, but in advisory panels in Washington, D.C. Matt had even read one of his books during his senior year. "Wow, nice job."

"Actually, it was," she said. "I had a nice apartment up on the hill in the Northwest section, off of Quincy Street. And I made some great money."

"Why didn't you head back to your apartment when you came into town?" he asked, then instantly knew it was a stupid question. "Never mind," he said, waving his hand and focusing on the boiling pot in front of him. "You don't need to answer that."

"No, it's all right," she said. "Paine, my fiancée, was staying with me the night before all of this happened. His body is still there, and I didn't want to see it again. At least not right away."

He looked up into her eyes. He could see there was still a lot of pain close to the surface there. He had topics like that as well. Both of them did.

"I'm sorry," he said.

She nodded and sat back. "Actually, I think the worst of it was that I couldn't bury him, or either one of my parents. I just didn't have the strength to move their bodies very far."

He nodded, remembering his parents and how hard that had been for him to do alone. "Yeah, I managed to bury my mother and father, but it took me most of a day just to move them to the small cemetery in Bend."

This time she looked deeply into his eyes. "Sorry, bad topic I guess."

"I don't think it hurts to talk about it," he said, putting plates, napkins, and some silverware on the table in front of her and in front of the other chair. "Considering that we haven't had anyone to talk to for three years about any of this."

"True," she said, smiling at him, "but not over a wonderful picnic lunch."

"Ahh, good point. Some topics just aren't meant for food."

"So how are we going to know if the bikers get close?" she asked, pointing at the security room.

"I have an alarm set that will tell us when they show up on a camera and set off a motion sensor. Same alarm that woke me up yesterday with you."

She smiled.

"Drink?" he asked. "I have chilled bottles of white wine I was going to bring along, but not sure now that would be a good idea. I have bottled water, Tang, cans of Diet Coke, and that's about it."

"Great thought on the wine," she said. "That would have been nice, but now I agree that this isn't a good time. Just water now."

He got them both bottles of cold water from the fridge, then drained the corn and put it on the table. He uncovered the chicken and rolls and then sat down.

"This smells wonderful," she said, waving the steam off the corn into her face. "I never thought I'd ever have another ear of fresh corn, let alone fried chicken."

She took an ear of corn, then a breast piece, a roll and two more deviled eggs. He watched as she bit into the chicken and her face lit up with sheer joy and pleasure.

"Fantastic," she said, looking up at him. "Thank you."

"No," he said, his smile so big it felt like it might break out of his face, "thank you."

Until that moment he hadn't realized just how much he had missed other people. Other *special* people.

And Carey was, without a doubt, very special.

EIGHTEEN

THE HOT SHOWER, the laundry, and now this fantastic-tasting chicken and corn. Carey would have never thought that such a thing was possible, let alone have it given to her by a guy with looks that seemed right out of a GQ magazine.

And besides the great looks, the superb body, and a smile that would melt a window, he had a wonderful personality, and actually seemed sensitive. He knew instantly when he had asked a bad question about her old apartment, even before she had said anything.

She was amazed that he had been worried enough about her to come and find her when he saw the bikers. He could have just let her go it alone, and she supposed most guys in his situation would have. She might have let him go it alone if the situation were reversed.

But Matt hadn't.

Was he too good to be true? Or was her ability to see another person just warped from three years of never seeing anyone?

She was going to have to be careful. She knew, without a doubt, that she could fall in love with him easily. And that was something she had never dreamed might happen again.

She didn't need, at the moment, to have another loss if he decided he didn't much care for her around. Even with them getting forced together faster than either one of them would have liked, they still needed to go very slowly.

Or at least she needed to go slowly. She had no doubt, that was going to be difficult.

After each of them had taken a few more bites of the wonderful lunch, Matt smiled at her. "So you still haven't gotten to the part of the story where you know what caused this disaster."

"You're right," she said, holding her second ear of corn in front of her mouth, "I'm falling down on my part of this bargain."

He laughed as she enjoyed the bite, then he went to work on a piece of chicken, ready to listen.

"I'm not sure where to start, exactly, so let me back into this a little. For a week before that last day, scientists around the world had been whispering among themselves about what seemed like a cloud approaching Earth. Actually Earth, and the rest of the solar system, was approaching the cloud."

"A cloud from deep space?" Matt asked, a chicken leg halfway to his mouth. "Sounds like a bad movie."

She nodded. "I wish it had been. But it was real. With the speed that Earth and the solar system were moving, and the speed of the cloud's movement, it would flash over Earth for less than five seconds. The problem was, no one was exactly certain what the cloud was."

"You're kidding?" Matt asked.

She smiled. "Actually, the leading theory was the

cloud was some sort of energy, visible only because of the light refraction it was causing to the stars on the other side of the cloud. Something out there was bending light, twisting it, ripping it apart, and Earth was going to pass right through that something."

"And no one told anyone this would happen?" Matt asked.

"There didn't seem to be a point. All the scientists believed that no one would notice anything. In fact, even on the night side of the planet, they thought that there wouldn't even be a glow in the sky from the wave."

"And your working with Dr. Canfield got you on the inside of all this information?"

She nodded. "His main lab was down near the river here in Portland. I was scheduled to work with him for the summer, and with luck, the fall semester. It made being with Paine hard at times, since the drive between Portland and Eugene is so boring, but we managed, making our time together special when we had it."

Matt nodded and said nothing. She wasn't sure if mentioning Paine again was such a good idea, but too late now, so she went on.

"Dr. Canfield's belief was that Earth was about to flash through a low-level electromagnetic storm. He had sent out a warning to others on his theory, to give them a chance to protect highly sensitive instruments. Strong electromagnetic pulses, like from an atomic blast, could shut down most modern equipment and destroy computers, but no one thought this wave was strong enough to do that."

"But they were guessing, right?"

"Yeah, we were all guessing." Her stomach twisted at the idea of how many people they might have saved if they had known. But they hadn't and there was nothing she could do about it now. She had already lost far too many nights to thinking about that.

"Dr. Canfield, to prove his theory, designed an experiment with two dozen sets of sensitive electronic equipment, to monitor the effects of the pass-through. Part of the experiment was to have one set of control devices locked in a secure vault, designed to protect anything in it from any kind of electromagnetic pulse. Some banks and some government military installations have such protections, developed back in the days of the cold war. It was easy for Canfield to set one up."

"Let me guess," Matt said. "You were in that vault, just like I was in the bank vault. That's what saved us."

She nodded. "I had worked two long days and nights on the experiments, side-by-side with Canfield, getting them ready. Then during the hour before the storm was to pass over, Dr. Canfield decided I should be closed in the vault with the control-equipment to monitor them."

"No one thought this thing might be dangerous to humans?"

"No one," she said. "Not one scientist in the thousands who were aware of the cloud approaching ever thought it would be dangerous. It was just a big, astronomical curiosity. It would be past Earth in seconds. Papers would be written about it. No big deal."

"Yeah, got that one wrong," Matt said, shaking his head.

"When I came out ten minutes after the cloud had passed, Dr. Canfield lay dead on the floor. From there, for me, as I'm sure it was for you, life became a pure nightmare."

After a moment of silence, Matt asked, "What did you do next?"

"I'm not really sure, to be honest. I think I was in shock. I remember stumbling around, checking for life in almost every body. Once I realized that was fruitless, I headed home, to my apartment. I found Paine still in my bed."

With that, the silence in the penthouse got very intense. She forced herself to take another bite of corn. Matt was nice enough to not say anything as she let the memory of that moment go past.

"I then made a nightmarish three hour walk over the hill and to Beaverton where I had grown up. My mother was slumped over the sink of our family home with the water still running. She had been preparing what looked like one of my favorite meals, corned-beef and cabbage. I moved her to the couch and made her look as peaceful as possible, as if she had fallen asleep watching television. Then I headed back into town."

"Why?" Matt asked.

"I wanted to find my father," she said. "He was in his office, slumped over his desk, his secretary on the floor in front of the desk. I managed to put him upright in his chair and turn it so it looked out over the city. At least his final resting place would have a view. I wish I could have done more for them."

"It just wasn't possible," Matt said.

She needed to keep going with this story, get it all out. She was amazed she had held her emotions together so far. She clearly was getting strength from Matt, and just telling this story to another human made her feel better.

"Finally, after a day, I managed to gather enough of my wits about me to think about what to do, where to go. I found myself at one point back in the lab. A part of the scientist-in-training in me took over. Since all the data had been recorded, the least I could do was try to discover what exactly had happened."

"Did you actually find out what in the cloud caused this?" Matt asked, sitting forward now, the picnic lunch between them ignored for the moment.

"I did. To be honest, the answer wasn't hard to find. The instruments designed to record and test Dr. Canfield's theory told me that he had been right, the storm was electromagnetic, but it had been resonating at the exact right band to shut down the human brain's electrical systems."

"Didn't know that was possible," Matt said.

"The military had been working on weapons using electromagnetic pulses for exactly that reason for years."

"Didn't know that, either," Matt said, shaking his head in disgust.

"I double-checked my findings, again coming up with the same answer. All the signals that are sent constantly from the human brain to the heart and lungs were short-circuited and simply shut off. In essence, everyone died before they even knew what had hit them. No one was in any pain."

"That's something good to know," Matt said, nodding. "Makes me feel a little better about my parents."

"Luckily, though, the storm's electromagnetic band had been very narrow. Over the years, I discovered it had killed all dogs, but not small cats. Horses are gone, but not cattle. Rats, mice, most rodents were killed, but not most fish. Deer survived as well. And raccoons. And a lot of bees and insects of different types. I have no idea of the long-term effects the massive disruptions in the food chains will have, and I really have no way of actually measuring why some animal's brains were short-circuited by the storm and others were not."

"Humans just drew the short straw," Matt said.

"They did," she said. "After one full day of doing that research, I had to escape."

She didn't mention to him that she had stopped and visited Paine and her parents on the way out, to say good-bye.

"I headed for the coast and now, three years later to the day, I came back."

"And I'm very glad you did."

"So am I."

Matt leaned back in his chair. "So, as I thought, the bank vault protected me, and the experiment vault protected you."

"Exactly," she said. "The electromagnetic pulse in the wave that hit the planet was weak, but sustained for just long enough to do this level of damage to humanity."

Matt leaned forward and stared at her. "Weak meaning what exactly?"

"Bank vaults would normally not have enough shielding to protect anything from a large electromagnetic pulse. Neither would the vault I was in. That means that just about anyone underground a good distance, or in any kind of military installation shielded for atomic blasts, would have survived. Or even someone behind a lot of metal."

"Oh, wow," Matt said, his gaze looking out over the city.

She watched him as he sat back and let what she had said soak in. Matt was clearly a very smart man and he had a common sense way of thinking that served him well. She admired that, wished she had more of it, to be honest.

"So, there might be a lot of people out there still

alive?" Matt said after a few moments. "Which is why it didn't surprise you when I said the bikers had plates from Nevada."

"Exactly."

"After being one of the only people around a city this size for so long," Matt said, "I thought there was no chance of ever finding a large group of humans again."

"Portland didn't have any military protected areas," Carey said. "We don't have subways, or military ships on the river. I'll bet there are more people in Seattle, a bunch more in California, and who knows how many in Colorado and Nevada."

"Subways, like in New York or Washington?" Matt asked. "You think there might have been enough to protect people? Or in submarines, or deep mines. Would any people in those have been protected?"

"Honestly, I don't know," Carey said. "But it wouldn't surprise me that they were. Was the bank vault door you were in open?"

Matt nodded. "It was."

"So even with an open vault, you and your co-worker were protected. I sure don't see why there wouldn't be others. Maybe a lot of others."

His eyes were alert, alive with the excitement of what she had told him. "Don't you want to know how many people might actually be still alive out there?"

"Discovering if people are still alive is the reason I'm sitting here, having this wonderful picnic instead of eating soup with my cats back on the coast."

Matt nodded. "I know you must miss your cats, but to be honest with you, I'm very glad you're here."

She stared at him for a long moment, then she said, "So am I."

NINETEEN

SHE HELPED HIM do the dishes, putting everything into a dishwasher, something she didn't have in the house she lived in at the coast. She loved his kitchen. It felt perfect for cooking, for conversation, for more than one person to move around another. The light from the big windows made it bright and the air-conditioning kept it cool.

While they worked, he asked her more questions about her job, about why she had become interested in physics, and about her years in college. It felt good to talk about those kind of things again.

Almost normal.

It seemed he craved just normal conversation as much as she did. That made sense after three years. When they were finished with the cleanup, the chicken covered and in the fridge along with the few remaining deviled eggs, she went back down the hallway to put her clothes in the dryer, then joined him in the security room.

She sat in her chair, pulling it up a little closer beside him. It was amazing how, in such a short time, she was really starting to trust this man. And enjoy his company, and being near him. She wanted to get a lot closer than they were, but so far she was managing to not show him that in any way.

He was being equally as cautious in return, something she appreciated.

"No sign of where they all went?" she asked.

"Nothing," Matt said. His fingers moved on the keyboard, showing different views of areas of Portland. All of them were empty. No red light was blinking on his big city map.

"Maybe they had planned on spending the night in the Hilton Hotel. There's also a lot of loft apartments and such in that area that would be easy to get in and out of."

"True," he said. "The old Benson is right across the street from the Hilton. If they're in that neighborhood, we might be able to catch a glimpse of them from the roof."

"You got some good binoculars?" she asked.

He laughed. "The best the stores had to offer. And a couple of telescopes too. One on the roof, one on the deck."

"I bet the stars on a clear night from here are wonderful," she said, standing.

"They are." He pushed his chair back and stood as well. "No lights of the city to get in the way anymore."

"Good point," she said.

He picked up a beeper-like device and held it up for her to see. "Remote alarm, to let us know if they're going somewhere else I have cameras. Or coming close to this building."

"You have all kinds of nifty gadgets," she said, watching him put it on his belt.

"Again, just too much time, an over-active imagination, and no limits on money. The no limits on the money is the key. It's amazing all the nifty devices man had come up with."

She had to agree with him there. Too bad all this invention and originality was now going to be lost in the ruins. She doubted that there was even enough of a population for man to survive, let alone survive in any real civilized fashion.

But she didn't say any of those depressing thoughts, instead she just followed him toward the elevator. Instead of pushing the button, he turned and went to a door off to one side of the entry foyer. "This is a private entrance to what had been a penthouse patio on the roof," he said. "Something extra for whoever lived in this place before me."

He opened the door and held it for her to go ahead.

"You have any idea who that was?" she asked as she started up the narrow staircase.

"Not a clue," he said. "I actually think the apartment might have been between owners, since there were no clothes, nothing in the kitchen, and everything looked cleaned and ready for someone else to move in."

"Lucky find," she said. "I had to clean out an older couple's things from the house I took over. Luckily, they weren't there, but it still wasn't fun."

"I bet," he said.

She reached the top of the stairs and pushed on through the heavy metal door. The heat hit her in the face like a hard slap. It was about noon, much hotter than this morning and even warmer on a rooftop. She wouldn't want to be up here around five in the afternoon when it would be hotter yet. She wasn't sure how long she was going to be able to stand this heat now.

They had come out on what looked like a stone patio, with a number of benches around one side, and what had been some planters, now full of brown weeds, marking the difference between the patio and the rest of the roof. Around her, over the waist-high edge of the building, the city stretched out around her, the river a blue band to her right, the mountains a green forest to her left. The sky was crystal clear, and the snow on the top of Mt. Hood seemed to just glow in the bright sun.

The maintenance building they had just come out of blocked her sight of the city to the south.

"Wow," Matt said. "It's turning into a real hot one today. I better check the garden."

He turned and went around a planter and out onto the gravel rooftop, heading toward the south side. She followed, her steps crunching on the gravel, moving slowly, very glad she wasn't spending the day out in this heat. In more ways than one, she had been lucky to have Matt find her. And being up on this hot roof was reminding her of that. His air-conditioning was a lifesaver.

She went around the corner of the elevator shaft structure and stopped cold at the sight. A lush garden stretched out in front of her, looking very out of place on the gray, gravel roof.

She shouldn't have been stunned by his garden, considering everything she had already found out that he could do. But for some reason, he just didn't seem to be a person who could grow things.

Yet he clearly was.

This guy really was too good to be true.

His garden stretched along the rooftop for a good fifty paces, and was twenty or so rows wide, filling the entire roof between the maintenance structure and the south edge. The planted area was framed by large boards at least a foot deep, forming what looked like a pool-like enclosure filled with dirt. Black rubber hoses of a drip water system ran along each row of plants and kept the ground a dark, rich brown, even in the heat.

"Amazing," she said, moving over and standing near where Matt was checking a water line. "Why did you build this instead of just going out and finding some ground somewhere else and planting a garden?"

"Seemed easier to have everything I needed close by," he said, moving to check a small pump, then working his way down a hose line. "And safer on a day like today."

She had to give him that.

She focused on the plants. From what she could see at a glance, he had about everything growing up here. Green peppers and onions were on the left. There were corn stocks, potatoes, zucchini, and a dozen other types of plants, some she didn't recognize.

"This is really amazing," she said. "It's bigger than my garden, and I have unlimited room. How did you get all this dirt up here?"

"One of those small tractors with a scoop on the front. It just barely fits in the service elevator."

"You're kidding?"

Matt smiled. "Nope." He bent over and checked another water line. Then he stood and smiled at her. "I brought it up here one scoop at a time from a spot down near where I saw you by the river."

She couldn't even imagine the amount of time that must have taken. He must have made a hundred trips at least. Of course, over the last few years, they both had nothing else to do but take care of themselves, so time wasn't an issue. But having the stamina to do something like this impressed her. Clearly Matt had a level of patience she didn't have.

She walked along the edge, watching him check the hoses, making sure everything was in place. When they reached the other side of the large garden, she was even more impressed. The thing was at least twice, maybe three times the size of her garden, and she knew how much time it took her to keep it going and alive. She just hoped most of her plants were growing when she got home. Even on the coast, it sometimes stayed dry for long enough to kill a garden.

"Can you grow enough on something this size to last an entire winter?"

"Well, here and on the twenty-first floor," he said, smiling sheepishly at her.

"Twenty-first floor?"

He shrugged. "Yeah, I have an indoor garden there as well, that I keep going all winter with lights. I like fresh vegetables, in case you couldn't tell."

"I guess so," she said, shaking her head.

He pointed toward a telescope sitting near the edge of the building on the north side, then started that way. She followed him, staring out over the city as he picked up the telescope, tripod and all, and moved it toward the west wall of the roof. "I've been trying to learn how to grow some spices down there as well, but not having much luck so far."

"They are tough," she said. "I can give you a few hints I learned from my mom."

"Would you?" he asked, clearly excited at the idea. "Anything to add a little flavor and change to the diet."

"I know that feeling," she said. "I've grown awful tired of fish and clams and crabs."

"Oh, don't I wish," he said. "I've tried fishing the river, but without much luck. Never really knew how to do it."

"Neither did I," she said, remembering those first few weeks of learning how to fish. "Books helped a lot."

"That's how I learned how to garden," he said, putting the telescope up next to the edge of the roof on the west side facing the main part of town and the hill beyond. "Gardening and elevator maintenance, right out of the books."

Just as he was about to look into the telescope, the beeper on his side went off.

He clicked it off, motioned that she should follow him, and headed for the door to the staircase. "Looks like some of them are moving."

She stayed right with him, matching him stride for stride all the way to the door. He opened it and held it for her, then she held the one at the bottom.

The air-conditioning in his apartment felt wonderful, and made her glad they hadn't stayed any longer on the hot roof. She was still not acclimated to this heat after living so long in the cool temperatures.

"Water out of the tap safe to drink?" she asked.

"It is," he said, moving toward the security room, "but grab a bottle from the fridge instead. And one for me if you would. It's colder."

"Got them," she said.

A moment later she joined him with the two bottles of cold water. "What are they doing?" she asked as she dropped into her chair.

"Nothing that I can see," Matt said, shaking his head. "The group downtown didn't set off the alarm. But this new group did."

"New group?" Her stomach twisted at the words.

On the monitor, she could see another large group of people on motorcycles, slowly working their way through wrecks on the I-84 freeway, heading toward Portland from the Columbia Gorge to the east.

They were dressed basically the same as the first bunch, in leather jackets, logical riding clothes even during hot weather. But from what Carey could see, these were mostly women, and some children. Only one biker in every group of five or so bikes was a man.

A couple of women had doubled-up on bikes, and there were three or four younger kids behind a couple of the men. One bike had a small sidecar with a woman in it holding a baby in her arms. That sight stunned Carey.

She kept staring at the woman and child until they went out of sight behind a large pile of wrecked cars.

"There are more in this group than the first group," Matt said, his voice low and sounding stunned. "Families and kids."

"And one with a baby," Carey said.

Matt nodded. "I saw that. Makes the entire bunch seem a lot friendlier, doesn't it?"

Carey had to admit it did. Seeing families traveling on motorcycles felt completely different than seeing a large gang of bikers in leathers.

"Looks like they're staying in groups of four or five bikes," Matt said, "with one person with a headset in each group, and one guy per group as well. The first group that came into town ahead of this one must be setting up living quarters. These folks are traveling smart. Very smart."

Carey stared at the woman with the baby in the sidecar as they came back into sight, moving slowly under Matt's camera position. "I wonder where they're from?" Carey said.

"Or where they're heading," Matt said.

"You think we should go talk to them later on?" Carey asked.

Just saying that thought out loud scared her more than she wanted to admit, and again she had to remind herself that the reason she was back in the city was to meet other survivors.

Again, her mother's voice echoed. *Such a brave little girl.*

Matt looked up at her. "I think we should wait until they get settled and decide then."

She could tell he was worried about the same thing. Yet she knew that since these were families traveling together, if they didn't take the chance to talk to them, find out where they were heading, they would both regret it later.

Suddenly, she had a thought that scared her even more. What they might be watching right here was the future of the entire human race.

"Good idea," she said, as more bikes came into sight. "No point in rushing into something and taking any extra chances."

Matt laughed. "Yeah, like I did yesterday meeting you. And like you did coming here with me."

She laughed as well, the tension easing. "Yeah, like that."

TWENTY

IN ALL HIS FEARS, in all his daydreams about finding other people still alive, Matt would have never thought it would happen like this, and in the way it was happening. First, Carey walked into town, a beautiful, smart woman, by herself. Then two groups of at least sixty men, women, and children on motorcycles.

After three years of seeing almost no one, this was feeling like too much. A small part of him just wanted the calm, day-to-day existence he had been living over the last two years. But now that he had met Carey, now that he had seen this large group of humans still alive, now that Carey had told him what happened to humanity, and there was a chance that there could be a lot of people left alive out there somewhere, he knew that he could never go back to that loner kind of life. And most of him didn't want to.

Most of him.

He and Carey spent the rest of the afternoon talking and watching the second group of motorcyclists work their way slowly into town. It took them almost twice as long to go the same distance as the first bunch, which explained part of the reason why they were not all traveling together.

But there were clearly other reasons, and Matt was very impressed at the organization and thinking that had gone into moving so many people. One bunch went ahead and set up camp, scouted for food, did what was necessary to find water and decent rooms. The leaders more than likely cleared out bodies from rooms, got water working where they could, found and set up generators, and so on.

The second, larger and slower group, came along as they could, finding a place to stay mostly ready for them when they got to the next stop.

It was also safer, Carey had pointed out. The first group made an imposing sight, and if they ran into trouble with someone already living where they were heading, the first group could handle it, or find a new campsite, without endangering the children.

If Carey hadn't already been there, Matt had no doubt he would have gone down and talked to them the moment he saw the second group coming in. He really wanted to understand better what they were doing, where they were heading, and why.

But with Carey beside him, he wanted to take a few less chances. He wasn't sure what he was feeling for her besides the natural attraction of a beautiful woman after three years of being alone. He was trying to keep that off to one side as best he could.

Most of the time, he was failing, but he was trying.

Carey wasn't making it any easier. She was fun to talk to, laughed easily, and seemed to be attracted to him as well. It was clear that she too was trying to move carefully and slowly when it came to him, which meant that a few times during the afternoon the conversation had been more like a dance.

In the middle of the long afternoon, after the group had completely made its way into the city and out of his camera range, he and Carey moved to chairs at the table, drinking sun tea and talking about their pasts.

He told her that he hadn't had a girlfriend three years ago. He learned about Paine, about Paine and Carey's engagement, and about her dad and mom and what it was like growing up an only child.

He told her about his family, and how his brother was living in New York.

They even told each other about their fears, and how they had coped with being alone, thinking they were the only person left alive, and how they had managed to both survive. Carey seemed very impressed by his travels that first year, and everything he had built here. He was impressed with how she had set herself up a safe home, learned how to use guns, learned many things from books. She had converted herself from a bookish scientist to a survivor and stayed sane. That impressed him a lot.

It was a wonderful afternoon of talking and sharing, one that he would have never dreamed he could have again with a woman. Or anyone, for that matter.

"You know," he said, glancing at his watch, "it has been over three hours since that lunch. How about I start an early dinner?"

He could see some hesitation in her eyes, as if suddenly the old habits of being polite, not imposing too much had crossed her mind. It was clear to him they needed to talk about the situation of where she was going to stay for the night, get everything out in the open.

He sat back and smiled at her. "Let me tell you how I hope things will go for the rest of the night, then you can tell me what you think."

Before she had a chance to reply, he started. "I would love to cook you a lemon-spiced chicken dinner, one I had planned just for me and Buddy originally. Fresh asparagus, corn, and bread as side dishes. Then, while there is still a lot of light, I'm thinking we might want to go say hello to the city's newest visitors. If we do it together, we won't look like a threat to them."

"Two against sixty," she said, laughing. "We're some threat."

"Good point. So, assuming all goes well with the visit with the bikers, we can come back here, have a late snack, maybe watch a movie. I have a few spare rooms back there that I have only used for light storage. We can set you up a bedroom, since it would seem a lot more logical for you to stay here, where it's cooler and cleaner."

"And don't forget safer," she said. "This alarm system of yours is heaven-sent as far as I'm concerned."

He smiled at her. "Thanks. To be honest, it would be great to have you stay. I've really missed having someone to talk to like we've been doing today."

She stared at him, a slight smile easing the corner of her mouth upward.

The silence in the room seemed to grow as they held each other's gaze. Finally, he couldn't stand it any longer.

"Okay, your turn."

"I would love to have a chicken dinner," she said, "if you allow me to help you cook it."

He nodded. "Deal."

She went on. "I'm scared to death about going down

there to meet those people for a reason I'll tell you over dinner. But I think you're right, we need to. A large part of me wants to find out who they are, where they are going, and so on. I would hate myself if I didn't before they left."

"Okay, that sounds—"

She held up her hand and stopped him in mid-sentence. "I would love to come back here and watch a movie as well. But only if you have microwave popcorn."

He laughed and pointed to the pantry. He had boxes of the stuff, and luckily, that stuff didn't spoil very often with time.

"And as far as staying here for the night in a guest room, I would appreciate that as well. I'm not doing too well in this heat, and having a cool bedroom for the night would make me feel a lot more like I was home on the coast."

They stared at each other for a moment.

She was smiling at him, and he could feel he was smiling as well. He really liked this woman. And the more time he spent with her, the more time he wanted to spend with her. It would have been that way, he was sure, even if the world was still out there beyond those big windows.

Finally, he pushed his chair back and stood. "Dinner and movie it is. And a visit to the neighbors in the middle. Sounds like a normal night to me."

She laughed and stood to help him cook. "Wonderfully normal. Just what the doctor would have ordered if he had lived."

TWENTY-ONE

CAREY WENT BACK to the roof and picked some asparagus sprouts for dinner while Matt cleaned and prepared the chicken. Then she got everything ready to cook the sprouts in a light oil with a little butter-salt flavoring added. It would only take a couple of minutes once the chicken was close to done.

Matt worked on skinning the chicken, then covering the four pieces in some sort of lemon herb sauce he had made. He slid the pan with the chicken into the oven.

"Thirty minutes until dinner. Potatoes next."

She peeled a couple of potatoes and got water boiling for them while he worked on a salad. While all this, they kept talking about anything that happened to come up. Gardening, cats, books they had read. To Carey, it felt wonderful.

She had never thought anything near normal was possible again. And as long as she didn't look out at the dead city too closely, she could let herself pretend they were just an ordinary, *very rich* couple in a penthouse apartment, cooking a summer dinner for themselves.

Right before everything was done, he sent her into the foyer near the elevator and told her to look in a closet there. Inside she found about fifty bottles of different Oregon wines, a couple of which were her favorites. She picked two whites, hoping that one would still be good after three years. Reds tended to last, but whites spoiled easily, depending on the length of time and how they were stored. So they might as well use the whites up first.

"You know," she said, carrying the bottles of wine back into the kitchen, "every Sunday for the past three years, no matter the weather, I've opened a bottle of wine."

"Really?" he asked, turning away from mashing the potatoes to glance at her.

"Corkscrew?" she asked.

He pointed to a drawer and she dug it out.

"Why only on Sundays?"

"It sort of marked the end of another week. And it was the only time I allowed myself to drink."

"Really, why?" He looked at her concerned.

"Don't worry," she said, "I don't think I have any problem with alcohol. I figured that the last thing I needed was to start drinking, and then have some really bad days and feel sorry for myself and drink even more. With an unlimited amount of wine and booze, it sure would be very simple to go down into that hole, make some stupid mistake while drunk, and end up dying alone."

He nodded as he filled a platter full of golden-brown chicken. She could tell he had had the same thoughts.

"After I buried my mom and dad up in Bend, I headed to a local bar I liked when I was home on vacations from college and proceeded to try to drink the entire bar's storeroom dry."

"Oh, man," she said, trying to imagine Matt drunk. "How long did that last?"

"I'm not exactly sure," Matt said. "I woke up under one of the bar stools, with a nasty hangover and hungry enough to eat a house. I haven't really had much more than a glass of wine since. As you said, too dangerous, especially when you're living alone."

She was very glad to hear that story. Both of them had learned to deal with living in the remains of the world in so many logical ways. It was good to hear that he had had trouble at the start just like she had had, and that now he didn't drink much. Both items made her like him even more than she already was, if that were possible.

The dinner turned out to be far too much food, even for two hungry people and a cat who seemed to eat anything. During dinner, she had told him about her friend getting beaten up by the bikers, and why just the sight of them had scared her so much. He agreed that made sense, but they both agreed that they still wanted to go together to meet the visitors.

"Okay, so how do we approach these people?" she asked as the last dish was put in the dishwasher and the counter wiped down. "I really don't feel right going up to them unarmed like you did to me."

Matt smiled and shook his head as he put a couple of wrapped up pieces of chicken in the fridge. "I don't either. I'm just glad you didn't shoot me."

"I'm glad I didn't shoot you as well," Carey said, smiling at him.

"I think we should just have our guns on our shoulders, and just walk up there not showing any threatening actions in any way."

Her stomach twisted. "It seems like we're taking a

pretty big chance. What happens if they don't like strangers?"

"Then let's just hope they turn us away without shooting first," Matt said. "I'm betting that people who have seen as much death as we have, and they have, are not really interested in seeing more."

She nodded. "Okay, seems like a better idea than trying to sneak up on them."

"Yeah, I agree there," he said. "And with that many of them, I doubt we could."

"So, we're off to visit the new neighbors. I've only been in the city one night and I already feel like they're intruding. I can't imagine how you feel about them. Or me, for that matter."

"Glad you're here," he said. "Mixed feelings about them. I'm just happy there are people besides me still left alive."

"With that, you get no argument."

They headed out to the foyer area. Before picking up any guns, Matt opened a drawer in a small desk sitting beside the closet and pulled out a metal object. "This is a spare key to the elevator. In case we get separated for any reason, come back here."

He handed her the key as if it were something he did every day, then turned to his gun rack.

She stared at the small, round key in her hand. He was really trusting her, completely, giving her access to his home and all his security. As far as he was concerned, they were together, at least for the moment. And she liked that.

"Thank you," she said, putting the key into her front pocket and then tapping the outside of her jeans to make sure it was securely there.

He slung a thirty-thirty rifle over his shoulder and

turned to smile at her. "You're more than welcome. Thank you for walking into my life. Let's just be careful now, shall we?"

"Sounds like a good idea to me," she said, putting her rifle over her shoulder. "How good a shot are you with that thing?"

"Expert with the sniper rifle," he said. "I can break a bottle on the river bank from the top of the roof here. How about you?"

"Good enough."

"That's perfect. Ready?"

"Almost," she said. "All right if I take a bottle of water with me? It's going to still be hot out there."

"Good idea," he said, "grab one for me."

When she got back into the foyer, he was standing there, holding the elevator door open for her.

"You know, in the old days, these things would start dinging in an annoying fashion when you did that," she said, getting on and handing him the bottle of water.

"I know," he said. "I hated that, so I shut off those alarms."

"You're very handy to have around," she said.

"Thanks," he said. "I hope to stay around."

She liked the sound of that a lot.

Thirty seconds later the elevator was again locked, they were across the lobby, and out into the heat of the early evening.

TWENTY-TWO

MATT REALIZED as they started up the hill on the hot sidewalk toward the Hilton Hotel that they had only guessed that was the area the bikers had gone to. Actually, considering how little of the city his cameras covered, they could be anywhere in a very large area.

"You know, this might take us some time to find them," Matt said.

"I don't think so." She reached out and stopped him, her hand on his bare arm, her touch soft wonderful against his skin. "Listen."

She was right. The sound of an engine running was clear, echoing down the street from above them. Then another one started.

"Sounds to me like they are right were we thought they might go," she said, taking her hand off of his arm and starting up the sidewalk again.

"It does, doesn't it," Matt said. He could still feel her touch against his skin, and for the moment that was all he could think about.

"How far do your cameras and alarms stretch in this direction?"

"Four blocks on the motion alarms," he said, "but

my cameras can see five or six more blocks than that up each street."

"And the Hilton is at least fifteen blocks. Good thing there's a lot of shade this time of the day."

"You going to be all right?" Matt asked, worried about her. It had occurred to him when they were up on the roof that she couldn't be used to the heat, not after spending the last three years on the coast, where a hot summer's day reached seventy.

"If I keep drinking the water, and we go slowly, I'll be fine," she said.

They moved along in silence for the next few blocks as the hill got steeper. Carey seemed to be having some troubles with walking up the hill on what had been a busy street and sidewalk three years ago. She was getting red in the face, and breathing harder than the slight hill should cause. After she spent an extra few moments staring at one body of a woman in what looked like it might have been a blue dress, he lightly touched her arm and pulled her into a shady alcove.

"Are you all right?" he asked.

"Not really," she said, trying to smile, but failing. She leaned back against the brick wall, staring upward at the sky.

"Memories?" he asked.

She nodded. "The three or four days after everyone died, I was still here in the city."

"Oh," he said, trying to imagine how bad that had to have been. "I left fairly quickly, headed for Bend. This place must have been awful."

"Worse than I want to think about," she said, clearly trying to catch her breath. "Front Street down to the Embassy Suites didn't have this kind of traffic on it, so it didn't bother me as much this morning."

"You want to go back?" he asked.

She shook her head. "No. I've been dealing with death for three years, walking around bodies in stores and on streets. This just brought back those first few days of memories is all. The sidewalks in the area around the lab where I worked were this crowded that day."

"Makes sense this would bother you," he said.

He took the bottle of water she had in her hand, opened it, and handed it back. "Drink."

After a long, gulping drink, she seemed to be doing a little better.

When he had approached Carey, she had come across as a tough, no-nonsense woman. As he learned more about her, he was coming to understand that she was just as afraid of this new world as he was, and had just as many issues dealing with it as he did. It didn't make her weak. The fact that she had survived showed just how strong and powerful she was. But having some trouble made him feel even closer to her, and they were getting close enough as it was.

"I wonder where all those folks on bikes spent that first year?" he said, trying to take her attention from the past to the present.

"I'd like to find that out," she said.

She held his gaze for a moment, then smiled, this time a real smile. "Thanks. I'll be all right."

"Of that I have no doubt," he said.

She took one more drink, put the cap back on the bottle. She pushed herself away from the wall. "Ready to go figure out who these new people are?"

"Ready," he said. "And I'm very glad you're with me on this."

She again stared into his eyes. After a moment she

reached out and touched his bare skin on his arm, sending a wonderful sensation through his body. "So am I. We seem to make a good team."

"That we do," he said, taking her hand and squeezing it lightly.

With that, they turned and kept going up the hill, walking side-by-side where they could. He liked having her beside him.

He felt stronger when she was there.

TWENTY-THREE

SOMEHOW, for the rest of the walk up the hill, she managed to keep the memories of walking around the days after everyone died in the background.

Such a brave little girl.

Someday, she was going to have to really get her mom's voice out of her head. She almost laughed out loud at that thought. Fat chance of that ever happening.

She focused on Matt, on the people they were going to meet, on staying alive and working toward some type of future. She wasn't sure what that future might be just yet, but right now a future felt a lot more possible than it did yesterday morning.

That thought almost made her laugh as well. Yesterday morning, her future was exploring a dead world and dying alone. Now she was in lust, maybe in love, with a man she had just met, and was about to walk into a crowd of bikers. Life after the end of the world certainly had taken a turn toward the interesting.

And hopeful.

Matt was giving her hope, showing her things she hadn't thought of before, and making her focus forward instead of backward at that day three years ago. She liked that about him.

She liked everything about him so far. He even had a nice ass. Could a man get any more perfect?

As they climbed the hill, she tried to ignore the heat as much as she could. The heat never used to bother her so much, and she knew the only way to get used to it again was to make sure she drank enough fluids. Beyond that, the only thing she could do was just not think about it.

The sound of a motorcycle starting up echoed through the buildings as they reached the lower east side of the Hilton building. The noise sent shivers down her spine.

Her mother's voice came flooding back once more. *Such a brave little girl.*

Shut up, Mother!

"Sounds like it's coming from just a block ahead," Matt said.

She nodded in agreement, but said nothing. She really wanted to take her rifle off her shoulder and hold it, but they had decided it would be better to just approach with the guns where they were. She wasn't sure if that was a smart idea, or one that might get them both killed.

He reached out and put his hand on her shoulder. "It's going to be all right. These really aren't bikers, like the old gangs. They're just ordinary people traveling in the most efficient manner possible, considering the conditions of all the roads."

She wanted to say, "We hope." But instead she just nodded and stayed beside him.

They reached the front corner of the Hilton and turned north.

She wasn't sure what she expected to see when they

found the group, but whatever her expectations had been, what greeted them was not it.

Not even close.

Instead of a street with skeletons and wrecked cars, the street had been completely cleared.

Completely.

A row of motorcycles were now parked down the middle of the pavement in a perfect row that seemed to stretch for two blocks. A couple of men on their backs were working under one that was idling.

The street, except without parked cars, looked like it had before everyone died. Someone had cleaned all the bodies off for as far as Carey could see. And moved all the cars. She had no idea why they would do that, but they had.

"Well, this is interesting," Matt said, voicing a massive understatement.

There were a couple dozen regular people walking back and forth from the front of the Hilton to the buildings across the street, not paying any attention to her or Matt. It almost looked like a normal day in the old city, as if she and Matt had suddenly gone back in time, and the city was alive again, instead of being a vast graveyard.

About fifteen people in all were in sight, doing various things. All of them had ditched their leather coats and were in tee-shirts and jeans, or light dresses. And unlike her, they all seemed comfortable in the heat.

She had to admit one thing. Without the leathers, they looked perfectly normal.

"No one is carrying a gun," Matt said softly as they kept walking toward the front of the Hilton.

He was right. Not even a pistol. In fact, most of the

motorcycles still had the rifles sticking up from slings or saddlebags.

A young woman in a light-blue print dress was the first to see them. She stopped, smiled and came toward them, no fear at all on her face.

None.

Carey felt like she might melt into a puddle of fear, but this woman looked as cool and calm as a receptionist greeting someone at an office door.

Carey figured the woman was about her own age, with a nice body that wasn't hidden at all by the summer dress and sandals. The woman had brown hair, cut short, and a dark suntan. She also had a large wedding ring on her finger, and diamond studs in her ears.

Carey was stunned at that. It hadn't occurred to her to put on either makeup or jewelry since the world ended.

As the woman got closer she said, "Hi, I'm Betty Ferguson. Are you two from here?"

"We are," Matt said, shaking the woman's extended hand. "I'm Matt Landel, this is Carey Noack."

Carey shook the woman's strong hand, but said nothing. Carey instantly liked this woman, and her forward nature, even though it wasn't the reaction she expected to have. She had come up here not wanting to like any of these people.

Matt couldn't seem to stop staring at Betty, acting like he had seen her before, or was stunned at her attitude, or something. Carey didn't know what to think of that reaction either. Was she going to lose the first man she had met in three years after just a day?

"Nice meeting you both," Betty said, giving them a smile that could stop any thoughts of problems. "We were wondering if we were going to meet some of the people already living in this area. You have time to talk?"

Matt glanced at Carey, then he laughed. "That's what we were hoping to do."

"Great," Betty said. "Come on. I think it's a little cooler inside. Dan and some of the others are going to want to meet you."

"Dan?" Carey asked as they headed toward the big front doors of the Hilton Hotel.

"Lieutenant Colonel Dan Houghton," Betty said. "He's sort of our reluctant leader at the moment, reluctant being the main word."

Betty held the door for them as they went inside.

Again Carey was surprised at how this group had, in a very short time, cleaned up the lobby. There wasn't a body to be seen, the floors had been swept, and the furniture dusted. If the large overhead lights had been on, the lobby would have looked like a normal day. Instead it was being lit by a series of lanterns set around the big space.

There were two men behind the front desk working on something under the counter. Both wore tee shirts, and one had a baseball cap on backwards to keep the bill out of his way.

"Hey, Steve, have you seen Dan?" Betty asked them as she got closer.

Both men looked up and stared for a moment at Matt and Carey. Then they both smiled.

"Local residents?" the man with the cap asked, then smiled again at Carey.

Carey caught her breath as the man's gaze held her. He was handsome in a rugged way, with a smile that showed perfect teeth, and green eyes that glowed, even in the lantern light. She was betting his name was Steve.

"Someone looking for me," a voice said from off to the left.

Carey and Matt turned to see a man in his fifties, with striking gray hair, walking toward them. He had the look of military, even though he was dressed in jeans and a casual shirt with the sleeves rolled up.

"Some of the local population has come calling," Betty said.

Carey wanted to say the only local population, but she didn't.

Matt stepped forward and introduced himself, then Carey. Carey shook the man's hand. She had hoped to meet new people coming into town, just not so many on the first day. After three years of being alone and talking only to her cats, this was getting overwhelming very quickly.

The man Betty called Dan seemed more like a father figure, or English professor, than a leader. He had a quick laugh, a smile that disarmed, and a deep voice. The most striking thing about him was his chiseled jaw, almost stronger than Kirk Douglas's jaw line.

Dan showed them back toward one of the ballrooms, where the smell of cooking dinner filled the air. They had cleaned out this big room as well, and the tables were in rows, with chairs in position. Clearly this was where they intended to have the group meals.

There was something about these people doing so much work to clean up this area that bothered Carey. If they were just traveling through, none of this would have needed to be done, or at least not to this extent. This group, as far as she could tell, was acting like they were planning on staying for a while.

She wasn't sure how she felt about that.

Dan took a chair across from Carey and Matt. Betty

joined them, along with the two men from behind the front desk, and two others. Dan introduced them all, but Carey missed their names completely. She had never been that good with names back in college, and now she wasn't even going to try.

Matt seemed a little surprised by all this as well. He made sure he sat close to her, his leg touching hers under the table.

"Well, sir," Matt said, starting off the conversation as everyone was getting settled. "You folks sure gave us a start coming into town like that today."

Dan laughed. "I bet we did. We scared a group so bad in Boise that they almost opened fire on us before we could convince them we were friendly."

"It's the motorcycles," Betty said. "It would scare me seeing a group like us coming."

Carey thought she might like Betty, now she was certain.

"So two big questions," Matt said, clearly wanting to direct the conversation at the moment. "Where are you coming from, and where are you heading?"

Dan glanced around. "Well, I'd say a large part of this group is from the Area 51 underground testing complex in Nevada, but Steve here, and a couple others, are from Colorado."

Then Dan faced Matt directly. "As for where we are headed, we're there."

Carey took a moment to realize what Dan had said. "Your destination is Portland? Why?" The idea of all these people staying here not only scared her to death, but excited her at the same time.

Dan sort of leaned back. "Let me tell you a story, if you don't mind, that might answer a bunch of these questions before I confuse the issue any more."

"Fire away, sir," Matt said.

"No sir, please?" he asked. "Just Dan."

Matt nodded. "Tell us a story, Dan. After what you said, I think Carey and I are all ears, so to speak."

Dan laughed, and then with a nod to Carey, started into his story.

TWENTY-FOUR

CAREY SAT AND LISTENED intently as Dan spoke, making herself breathe slowly and drink regularly. The last thing she needed to do was pass out from the heat or dehydration in the middle of his story. That would be rude, to say the least.

"Three years ago today many of us here," Dan said, "and about three hundred others still back in Nevada, were working the regular day shift in the underground testing areas in the base the press liked to call Area 51. Slowly, as the day went on, we came to realize something had gone very wrong on the surface. The few people that were up there had died, suddenly and without visible reason."

"How long did it take you to realize it was all caused by an electromagnetic pulse from space?" Carey asked, deciding to give the man something to think about right at the start of his story. She figured if that didn't knock him for a loop, nothing would.

Dan and the others stared at her like they were suddenly talking to an alien. You could have heard a pin drop across the large ballroom.

Then Dan laughed and broke the tension. "Actually, about a week, and it was the people in Colorado who figured out what exactly had happened. And remind me later to ask you how you knew."

Carey smiled at Dan and nodded. She had figured it was a good idea to let him know that she and Matt might be of use, just in case he had other ideas for them. Even though there was no sign of any problems from these people, the lack of trust was still there on her side, and so far she had seen nothing that major to change that feeling.

Matt touched her arm, a sort of signal that she had done just fine with her question. He let his touch linger for a moment, then pulled away. She wished he had left his hand there.

Dan went on with his story. "The base went into a heightened state of alert, thinking that the deaths were some sort of attack from some enemy. It wasn't until days later that we actually discovered it wasn't an attack on the United States, as the scope of the entire disaster was coming in from underground bases around the world."

"And from subs and big battleships and aircraft carriers," Steve added. "On the big carriers, everyone who was above the second deck or near an open port died. But the metal of the ships protected everyone down below. Those survivors had a real mess on their hands, because in one instance, everyone who knew how to navigate had died."

"That would mean that thousands and thousands have survived around the world," Matt said, his voice full of shock at the idea.

Carey was just as stunned. She had figured there might have been a lot, but after three years of seeing almost no one, that thought had faded to a distant dream.

"That's right," Dan said. "The electromagnetic pulse of the cloud that passed over the planet was just strong enough to short circuit the brains of everyone exposed, but not strong enough to penetrate too far underground, or through a certain thickness of metal. There are some guesses that up to a half million people around the world survived. Maybe more, considering how many people could be in subway cars or subway stations at the same time around the world."

"A half million?" Carey asked, her voice a whisper.

"Amazing, isn't it?" Steve asked, stating the obvious.

"The problem is," Dan said, "the half million are scattered everywhere over the globe, sometimes only one or two people in a large area."

Carey could vouch for that, but neither she nor Matt said anything.

"Everyone lost family, husbands, wives, parents," Dan said. "The shock was almost too much to allow any kind of order in any group to be maintained. For some people the loss just drove them completely crazy."

"I hear a large 'but' coming next," Carey said. "It's the *buts* that will get you in any story."

Dan laughed, the sound echoing in the big banquet room. "You're right. *But* after a while, people wanted to be with other people, and the groups started coming back together around the world, especially those in the military. Some of us had maintained a sort of order on the bases, not knowing what else to do. Slowly, survivors started coming back. We also had one big advantage. We had kept the power running which allowed the communication systems to function around the world."

"Makes sense," Carey said. After three years she had gone in search of other people as well, which had brought her to today, a day she would have never dared dream might happen.

"A lot of very good minds around the world survived the disaster," Dan said. "And those minds started working together to figure out how to best keep humanity alive without dropping back completely into the dark ages."

"At a half million," Carey said, "the human race will survive. No doubt there, but you're saying you wanted to help civilization do the same thing."

"Exactly," Dan said.

So far she was following everything Dan was saying, and was liking what she was hearing. So far.

Dan went on. "This group of scientists and planners figured that the best way to keep humanity alive and growing, and to hold somewhere close to the current level of technology, was to have as many people as possible gather in central places around the world, form towns and cities, salvage what could be salvaged, and focus on the future and education."

Matt laughed. "So let me guess, these people planning this went back to the basics on picking these central places, just as the pioneers did. The places had to have good natural resources like water and building materials, good growing seasons, mild climates, and so on. Everything Portland has."

"Exactly," Dan said, smiling at him. "Five spots in this country were picked. One area outside of Washington, D.C., for all the people who survived in the eastern corridor, one in northern Florida, another on the Mississippi River in the center of the country, a small town north of San Diego in California, and Portland."

"How many places around the world?" Carey asked, stunned at the scope of the plan she was hearing.

"Fifty-one at present count."

"Fifty-one," she said, softly, shaking her head. She couldn't even imagine that.

"And each place will be in contact with the others?" Matt asked.

"They will," Dan said, smiling at them. "Gathering places for mankind to rebuild, save what we can, and move on into the future."

Carey could feel the weight of being alone the last three years lifting off her shoulders. The death of Paine, her parents, everyone, had forced her into a way of thinking that had no hope, nothing but sameness, survival, and finally death alone. She had come into the city today hoping that wasn't the case, but knowing deep inside that it had to be.

Now this man was sitting her, telling her there was hope, there was a possible future, and that she could be a part of it. The relief was almost too much.

She took a deep, shuddering breath, and stared at her hands, trying to gain some sort of control.

Get it together, Carey.

Such a brave little girl.

Shut up, Mother.

Betty, who had sat down beside her, leaned over and put a hand on Carey's shoulder, patting it for a moment before letting go.

"Let me tell you what's going to happen next here in Portland," Dan said, ignoring the fact that she was having a moment of trouble. "Two more groups are coming in on bikes tomorrow. Those of us here already are going to spend the next day getting an area of the city ready for them, bringing in supplies, cleaning rooms, working on the water systems, setting up generators. We hope to have this two square block area livable in very short order."

"Then what?" Matt asked.

"We clear a two-way road from here to the airport," Dan said, "while continuing to clean up larger and larger areas of the city. Luckily, the bridges are still all in good shape, so no problem there. We just have to move all the wrecks."

"What are you doing with all the bodies you have to move?" Carey asked, looking up at Dan. She could just imagine these people taking a bulldozer and scraping the bodies into piles and burning them.

"We're giving every body the respect it deserves," Dan said, holding her gaze. "We're bagging each one and storing the bodies at the moment, including all the ones we took from this building, the street and sidewalks, and the buildings across the way. When we find the right area, and have the time, we will build a graveyard. We're leaving all the identification with each body, and where each body was found, so each grave can be marked as much as possible."

"That's a massive undertaking," Matt said. "I'm impressed."

"It was agreed by everyone in charge around the world that respect for the dead would be part of the system. The people that died deserve all the respect we can give them."

"I agree," Matt said, "but why go to that much work?"

Dan shrugged. "About all I can say is that it's the right thing to do, and a hundred years from now, our descendants will be glad we did what we are doing. There is already a central database set up in Colorado that will track where each person is buried when that starts happening."

"Everything looking to the future," Carey said, completely amazed that something like that would even be thought of, considering the magnitude of the task.

"Everything," Dan said. "At this point, the future is all we have."

"What happens at the airport?" Matt asked.

"Once we get it secure and working again," Steve said, taking over a moment from Dan, since it was clearly his area, "the rest of the people who choose Portland will start being flown in from Nevada, Colorado, and other areas. After that the airport will be used for what airports are used for now; transportation, shipping, and communications."

Carey nodded. Having contact among the major areas of settlement around the country and the world would be critical over the years.

"How many do you think will pick this city to start with?" Matt asked.

Dan shrugged. "We should have a population here, by the end of the year, of almost twenty thousand."

"Twenty thousand?" both Carey and Matt said at the same time.

The number sort of echoed around the room.

Carey couldn't even imagine that many people. Her mind just sort of stopped as she tried to grasp it and failed.

"And that should grow as more people who are on their own around the continent discover the five areas and move closer."

"Not everyone is going to join this idea, move into a city," Matt said.

"Of course," Dan said, nodding. "We expect there

to be smaller groups living all over the country, but the five cities picked will be the hubs of this country in a very short time, since they are where all the manufacturing and food production will be happening. Mankind can only scavenge from the bones of what is left for so long."

"I agree," Carey said.

Beside her Matt was nodding as well.

"So, now tell me," Dan said, staring at Carey and smiling, "if you don't mind, how you knew what happened three years ago today."

Carey laughed. "I don't mind at all."

For the second time that day she told her story of working for Dr. Canfield, who Dan, Steve, and Betty had all heard of. She told about the experiment, about how she survived, and about how a few days later she went back to the lab to find out what had happened, before heading to the coast to get away from all the death. She did not tell them where the lab was, however.

"Well," Dan said after she was finished, "What about you, Matt?"

Matt quickly told them what he had done before, and his background, being far too modest as far as Carey was concerned, but she didn't say anything. He also left out where he had been living.

"I sure hope the two of you will join our cause," Dan said. "We can use both of your skills, that's for sure. It's all volunteer, there is no pay besides food, since at the moment there is no money system in place. The work is hard and thankless at times, as I'm sure everyone here will tell you."

Across from Carey, Steve nodded.

"That's an understatement," Betty said.

Dan went on. "But at least, in my opinion, the long-term cause is right, and worth the effort."

"Thank you for the offer," Carey said, standing and offering Dan her hand. "I just need a little time to think about things first. This morning I was convinced I was one of only a few people left alive on the planet. All of this is going to take a little time to digest, if you know what I mean."

Dan nodded, his firm grip around her hand. "I do understand. This is a large planet and there are very few of us left in comparison to the numbers from three years ago. Many people will decide to go their own way, and that is fine. There is more than enough room for everyone, and certainly no housing shortage. Your choice is valid, no matter which one you make."

"You sure know how to say all the right things to a woman," Carey said, smiling at the man in front of her.

"I was married for twenty-three years," he said, laughing. "I should have learned, don't you think?"

TWENTY-FIVE

THE SUN WAS a distance below the hills to the west, and only the top of Mt. Hood was still in the bright light as they rounded the corner of the Hilton Hotel and started back down the street. The shadows of the buildings were deep, and so far there was no sign of a moon. Matt hadn't thought to bring a flashlight with them. They were going to have to be careful getting back. It was lucky they left when they did. Another fifteen minutes and they'd be walking the entire distance in the pitch darkness.

For the first two blocks down the hill, they walked side-by-side, not talking. Matt was going over what he had heard, how good it sounded, and yet how impossible it was to believe. From Carey's reaction in the middle of Dan's explanation, she was feeling huge relief that people were doing what they were doing. But she was also having doubts, he could tell.

If everything Dan had said was the truth, Matt felt the same relief that Carey had shown. But he wanted to wait, to make sure before offering to help turn Portland back into a city again. He had to admit this group looked good, and sounded good, but were they really what they claimed to be? A day or two would tell the difference on that. And he had a day or two to spare at this point.

"We need to be careful," Carey said, as they crossed the street two blocks below the Hilton.

"We'll go slow," Matt said. "Our eyes will adjust to the dim light and we'll make it before it gets too dark."

"No, I mean we need to be careful to make sure no one is following us," she said, glancing over her shoulder.

"So you're feeling like I am?" Matt asked, a little surprised at her statement. "We need to find out if this group is really doing what they say they are going to do, and if they are who they say they are, before we even get near them again."

"Exactly," she said. "We need to be careful about everything at the moment. I liked them, but not enough to just trust them with my life."

"I agree," Matt said. "And it just so happens I have something set up that might come in handy tonight. And give them a little test in the process."

He reached out and took her by the hand. He pulled her into the street, turning right at the corner, and leading them up the empty pavement. He loved the feel of her hand in his, and she certainly didn't complain.

"What are you talking about?" she asked.

He pointed up at the hill in front of them. Even in the growing dark, it was possible to see the homes perched up there, expensive in the days when a view really mattered. "I set up a generator and a locked house on the hill up there."

"Okay," she said, her voice low enough to not carry. "Why? I'm not following you."

"A decoy," he said, also keeping his voice low. "Two

blocks up this direction there is a large office complex that if we were heading up to the house on the hill on foot, we would naturally cut through. We'll start into that building, double back through a place I know we can't be followed, and then a few minutes later I'll light up the house."

"So if someone is following us, they'll think we went up there."

"Exactly," Matt said. "And we can see the area around it from the top of my building. And I have cameras and alarms rigged there as well."

She squeezed his hand and didn't let go. "Have I told you, in the short time I have known you, that I like how you think."

He laughed, leading them around a wreck. "You mean devious?"

"And careful," she said.

"That I am," he said.

He led her toward the office complex. A few minutes later they ducked inside the dark building and instead of going on through to the next street, they moved to the right down a narrow hallway that he had kept swept clear of dust to cut down on footprints.

Finally, going slowly in the pitch darkness of the hall, they got to a back door and went quietly out into the night. On a ledge there he picked up a remote control that would start the generator up in the house.

"Okay, now we be very quiet," he whispered, moving through the back alley and down the hill toward the street, keeping her hand in his. He had scouted this out, making sure there was nothing that he could trip on in the dark, and since it was getting very dark right now, he was glad he had.

At the edge of the building he stopped, keeping the

two of them against the wall, not willing to go out into the open again just yet.

"How long?" she whispered.

"It always took me about five minutes to climb the distance from this office complex to that house. I figure one more minute."

She squeezed his hand showing she understood.

He waited what he thought was long enough, then flicked the switch. From above the edge of the alley a glow lit the night, casting faint shadows on the buildings across the street.

"Drapes are pulled and everything," he whispered to her. "They won't know we're not in there."

He let go of her hand and eased out a little, checking the street in both directions for any movement.

There was no one that he could see.

"Ready?" he asked in a whisper.

She nodded and reached out and again took his hand. "Ready."

It took them a long thirty minutes to make it through the wrecks and back into his building, but by the time they got there, he was sure no one had followed them.

He wasn't sure anyone would have wanted to, but he felt a lot better being certain.

TWENTY-SIX

CAREY LET MATT lead her back into his dark apartment. She could just imagine that in the old days, the city would have lit up everything for as far as she could see from the penthouse, but now there was nothing but the outlines of buildings, deep shadows, and the faint pink of the last of the sunset on the top of Mt. Hood.

The coolness of the apartment felt wonderful against her face and arms after the muggy heat of the evening air outside. Just for the air-conditioning alone she was lucky Matt had found her. Not counting the fact that she doubted she would have worked up the courage to go talk to a bunch of bikers alone. More than likely, she would have seen them coming from a distance and just turned and headed back to the coast.

She had almost done just that. It might have been years before anyone found her, or before she might have tried to come back.

Matt was someone special. She had known that from the moment she had first seen him. And her attraction and respect for him had grown with every passing hour. He had treated her as an equal, while at the same time worrying about her, and giving her the use of his apartment for safety.

And as a team, they had gone to the group that came into town. She liked the feel of being beside him, working as a team. She hoped that would continue for much longer than one day.

She slid her rifle off her shoulder as Matt made sure the elevator was locked. "If you need to go down," he said, "use the key I gave you." He pointed to a spot over the top of the call button. "It fits in right here."

"Thanks," she said. "But I'm not going anywhere, except to the bathroom. I want to wash some of the sweat off my face and arms."

"I don't blame you," he said. "I'll take a turn after you. But we're going to have to keep the lights off for the moment," he said. "Can you find the bathroom down the hall in the dark? After the door is closed you can click on the light."

"I can find it," she said, gently touching his arm as he came up to her.

"I'm going to check to see if anyone followed us here, or up to the decoy house," he said, taking her hand and holding it for a moment.

Then he let go and set off through the shadows of the apartment toward the faint light coming from the electronics room, leaving her alone in the semi-darkness.

She let the feeling of his touch linger for a moment longer, then managed to get down the hall to the bathroom. Less than five minutes later, she made her way back through the apartment to the security room without kicking any furniture, or banging her toe on any corner.

Buddy sat in the door of the security room, the faint

light from the monitor framing him like an Egyptian god.

"You waiting for me, Buddy?" she asked, bending down and extending her hand in an offer to pet him. "Or guarding the room?"

Buddy leaned forward into her palm, letting her scratch his ears, telling her clearly that he had been waiting for her to come and do her duty in worshipping him.

"You really are a cat person, aren't you?" Matt said, turning around in his chair to watch her and his cat.

"I am," she said, "and I miss mine. I'm glad Buddy is giving me a little cat fix."

Matt laughed, clearly in a good mood. What he had seen on the screen had encouraged him, that was for sure.

"No one followed us?" she asked.

"Not a sign of anyone," he said. "I don't think any of those people have moved out of that two-block area since they got into town. A deer set off one of my motion sensors off of I-5 an hour ago, but that's about it. With this system, I could never tell there were so many people in town."

She sat on the floor in the doorway so that she could keep petting Buddy. Then she stared up at the monitor and all the green lights on Matt's security map and tried to make some sense out of all this.

"Okay, if I remember right, there's a grocery store close to the Hilton," she said.

"There is," Matt said.

"So with that, and both hotel kitchens, and the nearby restaurants, there would be enough supplies left in those storage rooms to feed those people for a long time. Am I right?"

"You are," Matt said. "And from the smell that was coming from that kitchen off the ballroom, the group probably brought in their own supplies as well, maybe from game they shot along the way."

She nodded. That group didn't need to go anywhere for food, at least for the night.

"They just ignored us after we left," Matt said. "I don't think I could have done that in their position."

"Then it's clear they weren't real worried about the two of us," Carey said. "Why?"

In the light from the monitor she could see Matt shake his head. "I honestly don't know. I'm slowly starting to believe they are doing what they say they are doing. But even that makes no sense. They are in a new place, yet I didn't see any guards as we approached, or left. Did you?"

"Not a one," she said. "And no one had a gun. They didn't feel it was a priority, even though we carried guns walking into the middle of them."

"Which can only mean they are very secure that there are no dangerous groups of people in this area," Matt said. "How would they know that? My security systems would have seen any advanced scouts they sent into the city, and there just hasn't been any."

Suddenly, it dawned on Carey how those new people would know she and Matt were no danger. After three years, she had already forgotten what century they were living in.

"Satellites," she said, laughing. "I bet they know where every person in this entire area lives. If you had the kind of resources they claim they do, and were planning on moving twenty thousand people into an area, wouldn't you scout everything out first?"

"Of course," he said, shaking his head and laughing.

"And most of the spy and weather satellites would be working just fine after three years." He laughed. "It seems our thinking has gone backwards in three years."

"That it has," she said. "It felt odd today even thinking about electromagnetics again. Three years ago that was just about all I thought about."

He reached over and picked up the radio-controlled remote. "No point in keeping the lights on in the decoy house. I have a garden on the roof here. They know exactly where I live, and more than likely, what vegetables we had for dinner."

Carey laughed. "No wonder they weren't surprised when we showed up. They probably got word we were on the way."

"And they sure didn't need to follow us home on the ground tonight," Matt said.

"I'm starting to think these people are the real thing," Carey said. "Their story sure sounds logical on the surface. And they are being very consistent with the story."

"And three years is about the right amount of time that it would take for everything to fall apart, then groups to get back together and start working on something like this."

"True," she said, giving Buddy a good scratching under his chin. His purring was filling the room. "And as you said, Portland is a logical place to start over because of the resources here."

"So what do we do now?" Matt asked, sitting in his chair watching her pet his cat.

She smiled at him, noticing how handsome he was even in the dim light. "How about that movie you promised me. And the popcorn. We can talk about the rest of this tomorrow."

"Perfect idea," he said. "But you're going to have to help me pick out a movie."

"Something classic and pure escapism," she said, pushing herself to her feet slowly. The long day was starting to catch up with her. She could feel the exhaustion creeping into her mind. It was hard to fathom how much had happened today, yet she didn't want the day to end just yet.

"All right," he said. "Popcorn is in the pantry. I'll get the movie if you get the popcorn started."

"Deal," she said. Again he was treating her like a partner and she liked that. She liked that a lot, actually.

"I'll reset the alarms here on the security system, just in case anything comes into the area," he said. "But I have to warn you, my nighttime alarms are louder than the day ones."

"Oh, joy," she said.

He laughed as she moved back into the darkened living room area. A moment later he flipped on the lights.

"Wow, those are bright," she said, shading her eyes as she smiled at him.

"They will dim for the movie," he said, "I promise." He went past her toward the elevator foyer.

"You're not going outside to get a movie, are you?" Carey asked from the kitchen area as he reached the elevator and unlocked it.

"Nope, just down a floor," he said. "I have two rooms downstairs full of movies."

"On the same floor as your second garden?" she asked, smiling at him.

"Just across the hall," he said, as he got onto the elevator and the door closed.

She went over to where her backpack leaned against

the wall and kicked off her shoes. Then she took her socks off and stuck them into a pocket of the backpack. Her feet had been hot all day. She would apologize to Matt if they smelled, but she needed to get out of those shoes.

The tile floor of the kitchen area felt wonderful on her bare feet as she got two packets of microwave popcorn out of the pantry and started one.

Then she stood and looked around. With the lights on inside and the windows and city around them dark, she got a much better feel of the immense size of this place. Yet even with the size, it was still comfortable.

The apartment was clearly Matt's, yet she felt at home here, as if she had lived here at one point. She had never been in another person's apartment where she felt this good, this at home. Even Paine's apartment in Eugene was always just Paine's apartment, and when she stayed there with him she had always been the guest. And Paine had said he felt the same way about her place. When they got married they had planned on finding a new home and furnishing it together, to try to make it their place.

But Matt's apartment was another matter, and she couldn't put her finger on exactly what it was, other than Matt himself. She just felt safe and comfortable with him, and he made her feel completely welcome in his home in his every move.

The first bag of popcorn had just finished when the elevator door opened and Matt came out carrying a movie. He locked up the elevator again as she put in the second bag.

"I love the smell of that stuff," he said, flipping the DVD onto the counter in front of her.

She picked it up and then smiled at him, not believing that he had picked one of her favorite old movies. Audrey Hepburn, Gregory Peck, Eddie Albert, in *Roman Holiday*. A movie about two people meeting and escaping from their real lives to fall in love. She loved this old movie and, almost as much, the modern remake called *Notting Hill* staring Hugh Grant and Julia Roberts.

"That all right?" he asked, grabbing a bottle of pop and opening it, smelling to make sure it hadn't spoiled over the years. "You did say escapism and classic remember?"

She laughed. "It's one of my favorite movies. I could watch it over and over. And have. And would love to do so again tonight."

"It's one of my favorites as well," he said, starting toward the living area with two glasses of pop. "Bring the movie and the popcorn."

She did as she was told, putting the popcorn on the coffee table in front of the couch, right beside where he had put the two glasses. He took the movie and indicated she should get comfortable on the couch.

The sofa was as soft and inviting as it looked, and she sank into it with a sigh.

"It's been an amazing day, hasn't it?" he said as he put the movie into the player and then moved to dim the lights.

"It has," she said, watching him come toward her. "Thank you."

"For what?" he asked, sitting on the couch beside her and picking up the remote.

"For everything," she said, not really knowing what to say or how to say it. "For trusting me, inviting me into your home, giving me a chance to see there might be a possible future for all of us left."

"After three years alone," he said, turning to look into her eyes, "I'm finding it hard to grasp that I might not have to be alone any more. Aren't you?"

She laughed. "I'm having a hard time grasping I've met you, let alone that there might be hundreds of thousands of people left alive out there."

"Yeah, me too," he said.

He picked up his bag of popcorn, sat back on the couch, and started the machine. "Then let's watch a movie and give all this time to sink in."

"I love the idea," she said, taking her bag of popcorn and settling back beside him.

She was sitting on a couch, watching a movie, with a man she hadn't even known yesterday morning, let alone believed existed. Yet she felt completely comfortable with him, and very attracted to him. Just having him beside her felt right.

By the time a quarter of the movie was over she had put her popcorn aside and was leaning against his strong shoulder.

Sometime before the middle of the film she could no longer keep her eyes open.

The next thing she knew, Matt was moving her, stretching her out on the wonderfully comfortable couch, putting a pillow under her head and a soft blanket over her.

"If you need something," he whispered to her, brushing her hair off her forehead gently, "you let me know."

She was so tired, all she could do was sigh and nod under his soft touch. What she really wanted was for him to fall asleep beside her, holding her.

But she didn't even have enough energy to ask.

TWENTY-SEVEN

MATT WASN'T SURE who fell asleep first. All he remembered was that he woke up and the sleep mode on the DVD was floating a logo around his screen like an old pong game. The room was silent, the air almost chilly.

Carey was curled up against him, her breathing regular, her head against his arm. He had been sleeping with his head on hers, leaning toward her, the two of them holding each other up. Her hair was soft and smelled of raspberry shampoo. He pulled away slowly, making sure to not pull any of her long brown hair.

She was as beautiful in sleep as awake. Her face was peaceful, her light skin smooth. He studied the lines around her eyes, her eyebrows, her soft lips, her faint freckles, trying to memorize every detail. Her mouth was slightly open, and the feel of her soft breath was wonderful against his neck and face.

He wanted to take her in his arms and hug her, but he refrained. The last thing he needed to do was scare her. They had only been together a short time, and considering everything they had both been through over the past three years, falling asleep together was a great trust on both their parts.

He eased himself away from her, leaving her sitting for a moment with her head on the back of the couch, breathing softly. Then he clicked off the television and went for a blanket and pillow.

He got the pillow in position on one end of the couch, then gently eased her head down, covered her, and brushed the hair from her face, enjoying the touch of her smooth skin against his fingers. She was so beautiful, all he wanted to do was kiss her and crawl in beside her and hold her. But it wasn't the right time, and he knew it.

She awoke a little, but didn't object to being stretched out on the couch. She was asleep again before he walked away.

He turned off the dimmed lights in the main area, leaving on only the hall light so she could see where she was when she awoke, and could find the bathroom again. He had planned on making up a place for her to sleep in one of the spare rooms, but for the moment, the couch would work just fine. Over the last two years, he had spent many a night on it, and he knew it was comfortable.

He barely made it to his own bedroom, got his clothes off, and crawled in before he was back asleep as well.

The next thing, he knew the sun was lighting up the city outside his large bedroom window, and his security alarm was going off, the loud beeping more annoying than any alarm clock could ever be.

As always, it took him a moment to realize what it was.

"Damn deer," he said to himself. He crawled out of

bed, nude and headed for the door. He got a half a step into the hallway before he remembered he had a guest.

Carey!

His world had changed, and changed drastically. And more than likely this alarm wasn't a deer, but more of the group coming into town.

He had not been jolted so awake, so fast, in a long time.

It took him a long few seconds before he could pull on a pair of exercise shorts and a sweatshirt and get out of his room again.

The couch in the living room was empty, the blanket folded under the pillow on the coffee table. A glass of orange drink sat half-full on the counter top.

Carey must have already been up when the alarm sounded. Her backpack and rifle were still against the wall near the elevator, so she hadn't left. That realization made him feel even better. He didn't want her to leave.

He headed for the security room. Carey was in there, shaking her head at the monitor, sitting on the chair they had moved there for her yesterday. Her hair was wet and she had on clean clothes.

"Morning. What's happening?" he asked, dropping into his chair and trying to make sense of the images on the monitor.

"Sorry, I couldn't figure out how to turn off the alarm," Carey said over the noise. She smiled at him, sort of a fond grin. He realized he must look a mess. Most of the time he awoke in the morning with his hair going in all directions and he had no doubt this morning would not be an exception.

"Right here," he said, punching off the alarm and then running a hand through his hair to try to smooth some of it down. He was going to need a shower as well.

The alarm that had been triggered was on the Chambers Street exit off of I-405. A dozen people were working their way along the wrecks blocking that exit and off ramp, and along the area on the freeway below the exit. They were opening the car doors and putting the bodies, clothes, purses, and all, in black garbage bags. They even emptied the glove boxes of the cars into the bags and checked the trunks.

Matt stared in shock. They were doing as they had told them they would do. The bodies were being treated carefully, and the bags, once sealed, were put in certain areas beside the road.

Up at the top of the exit, where they were clearly done with the body removals from the cars, a large bull-dozer was shoving the wrecks to one side, clearing the street. Matt remembered that same bulldozer being down on a construction sight about four blocks east of the Hilton. These people had people who knew how to operate heavy equipment, and get it started again after three years. They had come prepared, that was for sure.

Three others were loading the body bags into a pickup truck. Another pickup quickly took over as the first left with its load and disappeared out of the camera range.

"They're starting on the road clearing to the air-port," Carey said. "It sure seems that what they were telling us was the truth."

Matt just stared, nodding. "It does seem that way, doesn't it?"

They sat and watched. Matt didn't know what to think, other than he had to use the bathroom and take a shower.

He turned to Carey. "Nothing we can do now but watch and think about our choices. But first I need a shower, then some breakfast. I have more eggs and all that stuff. You up for that omelet I offered a few days back?"

"I'd love one," she said. "You take your shower, I'll get out the supplies for breakfast and get started."

"Good idea," he said. They stood and headed for the kitchen.

"You sleep all right?" he asked, stopping in the hallway and watching as she opened the refrigerator door. "I'm sorry we didn't get a bedroom set up for you."

"The couch was great," she said, pulling out some eggs and placing them on the counter. "If I had one that comfortable in my place, I'd never get off of it."

"I know that feeling," Matt said. "I spent many a night on that thing, too tired to even bother to get up and go to bed."

"Climbing poles putting up cameras will do that to you," she said, laughing. "Now go get that shower before we both starve to death."

He smiled at her, then turned and headed down the hall, the sounds of another person in his kitchen the most wonderful noises he had heard in over three years.

TWENTY-EIGHT

WAKING UP on Matt's couch had been a shock.

The sun was bright in part of the room, flooding the entire main area with more light that she thought possible in a room. It had taken her a moment of squinting to remember exactly where she was.

She had climbed off the couch and looked around, checking out everything, including her backpack, making sure it was still where she had left it. She didn't expect it to be moved, but after living alone for so long, she found it hard to trust anyone. Even Matt, no matter how much she was attracted to him.

The apartment was quiet, the sun already high in the east over Mt. Hood. She stood, staring at the fantastic view for a moment, then turned and headed quietly down the hall. The first bedroom was Matt's and she glanced in at him through the open door, feeling a little like a peeping tom as she did so.

He was breathing evenly, not really snoring as he lay on his side. He had one bare leg thrust out from under the blanket. She stared at his bare skin, wanting to touch it.

There was something about this guy that hit her

buttons. More than just about anything, she wanted to be in his arms right at that moment.

Or maybe that was just anyone's arms.

Snap out of it, Carey.

Three years was a long time to go without other human contact. She wasn't sure yet if it was Matt she wanted, or just the companionship. Better she have a very clear answer on that before she moved any farther with him.

Buddy lay on the corner of the bed. The cat looked up at her, its eyes half-closed, then laid its head back down and went back to sleep.

Damn she missed her cats. Both of them slept with her as well every night. She was going to have to get back to the coast soon and see how they were doing.

She stood there in his door, silently staring at him, studying the lines on his face, the messed up hair, how he held his mouth. She really was attracted to him, more than she remembered being attracted to Paine.

Far more.

She wondered what he would do if she took her clothes off and just crawled in beside him. More than likely he would welcome her. But it didn't seem right, no matter how much she wanted to.

Actually, it seemed very right, just not yet.

Finally, she forced herself to move on into the bathroom, picking up a fresh change of clothes from the dryer as she went.

She took a long, hot shower, letting the water drain the tiredness and worry from her muscles. Then she put on clean clothes and headed back for the kitchen, glancing in at Matt as she went past.

He was now laying on his back, his mouth open, snoring softly.

She could sleep with that level of snoring.

She shook her head, surprised at the thought. Everything seemed so normal with him there sleeping like that.

Again, she considered crawling in with him, then forced herself to move away.

Go slowly. You've only known him for two days.

It seemed so much longer.

She went back into the kitchen and made herself a fruit drink. She was sitting at the counter, staring out at the city when the security alarm went off. It sounded like a cross between a really loud buzzer on an alarm clock, and the siren of a cop car. The apartment had been so silent, the sudden noise startled her, making her heart pound as she looked around trying to figure out what it was.

"Security alarm, dummy," she said as she headed across the apartment.

"Damn deer," she heard Matt say from down the hall as she got to the security room where the alarm was coming from.

The moment she got inside the security room, she knew it wasn't deer, that much was for sure.

She dropped into her chair, searching for any obvious buttons or switches that would shut off the loud alarm. She couldn't see anything, and after a moment figured it was just better to not touch anything. Matt was going to want to see this.

He came in a moment later and dropped into his chair. He had on shorts and a baggy sweatshirt that looked like he had done gardening in it. His hair was sticking out in all directions, and he had a sheet mark crease across one cheek. He looked so damn cute, she just wanted to hold him.

She apologized for not being able to shut off the alarm as he silenced the awful racket, then they spent the next ten minutes watching the new people work clearing the road. The fact that the newcomers were actually treating the bodies from the cars and sidewalks well gave her a feeling that Dan and the rest had their priorities in the right place and really were looking to the future. With so many dead, it would have been easy to just push them aside, worry about it later, after the living were taken care of.

But not this bunch.

They seemed to know they were going to succeed, that there was going to be a new world coming up out of the ruins of the old one. And because of that, they were treating every body from every car, from every building, like a fallen war hero, putting the bones and clothes and personal effects in bags and handling the bags with respect. The future, if this all worked and the human race survived, would be very glad this was done the way they were doing it.

She doubted the new people knew she and Matt were watching. This was just the way they were going to work, as Dan had told them they would last night.

That gave her a vast amount of hope for the future. At least far more hope than she had held at this time yesterday morning. So much, in fact, that she didn't even want to say anything.

Finally, Matt suggested he take a shower and then cook them both breakfast, which she had readily agreed to, since her stomach was rumbling and his offer of omelets that first morning had sounded fantastic.

He went off to shower, leaving her to get things started in the kitchen. By the time he got back, wet hair combed into place, she had chopped up some onions, a green-pepper, and cut some bread left over from dinner for toast.

She had been right about the feel of his kitchen. It fit her, as if she knew where every utensil, every appliance was before she actually found it. It was exactly like something she might have designed for herself. Maybe better.

Within minutes they were sitting at the table eating breakfast like a normal couple after sharing a night and a life.

She and Paine had had a few of these types of mornings. Usually they had been on a Sunday, when they both sat and read the paper, sharing different things that interested them. There hadn't been many of those mornings with their work schedules and school. Not near enough.

Now Matt sat across from her, staring intently at her as she ate.

"What?" she asked, using a napkin to wipe off her mouth. "I have egg on my nose or something?"

He laughed. "No, just sitting here thinking about how beautiful you are, and wondering what you were thinking about."

She could feel her face blush slightly at his compliment. "Thank you," she said. "But actually I was thinking about how nice this felt having breakfast like this, and how Paine and I hadn't gotten the chance very often to do it."

"I'm sorry," Matt said, the smile instantly gone from his face.

Oh, damn it all, she had screwed up. She held up her hand. "No, no, it's all right. I know Paine's gone and there's nothing I can do about it. I just meant that this feels nice is all."

"It does, doesn't it," Matt said, nodding.

He took another bite of toast covered in raspberry jam, then looked at her with a very serious look. "You know, we can bury Paine and your parents, if that's what you'd like to do. I'll be glad to help."

She smiled at him. His offer was very kind, and from what she had already seen from this man, not unexpected. Clearly Matt had a very big heart.

"Thanks," she said. "That's very kind. Maybe at some point down the road, after we figure out what to do about those people out there, and Dan's offer for us to join them."

Matt nodded. "What are you thinking about the offer?"

"That I need more information," she said. "I'd love to know what being part of what they are attempting would mean for me. And their expectations. And if I can even be of help."

"Exact same questions I was wondering about," he said. "I'm having fewer and fewer doubts about them being what they say they are. Especially after this morning. This city is going to be a very different place when twenty thousand or so people show up."

She looked out at the sea of empty buildings. "It will come alive a little, that's for sure," she said. "If they have the ability to get that bulldozer working, I bet they have the type of people with them that could start up the hydro-plants up on the Columbia, and get the power flowing into the city again."

Matt laughed. "Yeah, and picking Portland was a good choice as far as the water goes. The system that brings in the water from the Bull Run drainage up in the hills is more than likely just fine. With power, it will be very easy to clean and get back up to standard. But it's going to take a lot of people going around and turning off water faucets left on three years ago."

"Maybe that's what they want us to do," Carey said, and laughed. But she was half serious. With her background, she really didn't have anything practical she could offer in building a new society from the rubble of another. Matt, on the other hand, would be a golden find for them considering all his skills.

"Why don't we just go ask them after breakfast?" Matt said. "Before it gets too hot out there."

"You know," she said, taking the last bite of her omelet, "I think that's a splendid idea."

"I'm glad you do," he said. They held each other's gaze for a moment before both began laughing.

Twenty minutes later they had cleaned up the breakfast dishes and were headed down the elevator. Both of them still had rifles slung over their shoulders, but Carey doubted they needed them.

TWENTY-NINE

CAREY WAS VERY GLAD that Matt had suggested they go out early, before it got hot. It was still only around nine in the morning, yet the air was starting to turn warm, and she could feel that the wind was from the Columbia Gorge, which meant it was going to get much, much warmer.

It didn't take them long to get back up to the Hilton. And for some reason, the knowledge that all the bodies in the cars, and on the sidewalks, would be taken care of at some point in the future, made it easier for her to move among them. It still brought back the memory of that first day, but the memory didn't eat at her as bad, wasn't as close to the surface, as it had been the night before.

She would never forget that day, and the days that followed. She doubted anyone left alive ever would. But at least she might be able to deal with it better now.

Amazing how focusing on the future instead of the past could change an attitude. She hadn't felt this good, this positive in three long years.

There were very few people around the Hilton, and even fewer inside. Amazing how sixty people could just seem to vanish into the buildings and empty city.

They finally found someone who thought that Dan might be in the communications room. She and Matt were directed to a building across the street, an office building, and then upstairs to what must have been a large, second floor meeting room.

One wall of the room had been filled with communications equipment of different types, filling a dozen different shelves. It was an impressive display that clearly hadn't been there yesterday. Matt stopped and stared for a moment.

The large sliding doors at the end of the room were open. Carey could see a couple of satellite dishes on the balcony outside. And other wires going out another open window and leading up to the roof.

Dan was sitting at one conference table, talking to a man about something to do with an uplink, while two other men worked on equipment. Carey could tell by the way Matt moved slowly from one shelf to another that he was impressed at the set-up.

"Wow, you folks really know what you're doing," Matt finally said.

"Not really," one man said. He was on his back, under a large piece of equipment, and he sounded disgusted. "More like we're making it up as we go."

Matt laughed. "Boy do I know that feeling."

Dan looked up from his conversation and smiled at them, standing and moving toward them. Carey could tell the smile was real. He was actually very happy they were there.

"I was hoping you two would come back," Dan said. "More questions about what we're doing, I assume."

Carey was shocked at how much she liked the older

man, and felt comfortable around him. When she had worked with Dr. Canfield, she had had to deal with a few military types. They were always nice, but they had made her uncomfortable. But Dan put her at ease just with a smile.

"More questions," Carey said, agreeing.

Dan motioned them over to a few chairs near a fairly empty table. Then, after they were all seated, he said, "Ask anything. We could use both of your help, so I'll give you as much information as I know. Straightforward, no punches pulled. How's that?"

"Sounds good to us," Matt said, glancing at Carey.

She nodded and let Matt start the questions.

"First off," Matt said, "How do you know you could use our help?"

Dan laughed. "Fair enough. We knew there were a few people living in this area. After you came by last night, I got in touch with our main base back in Nevada." He pointed to one of the machines near the window. Carey had no idea what it was, but from the way Matt nodded, he must have had an idea.

Dan went on. "I gave them your names, and they, in turn, contacted Colorado where there is a vast storage area of information about people around the country."

"And our names were in that database?" Carey asked, clearly amazed.

"They were," Dan said, nodding. "Of course, this data was meant to be for people working on family trees on the Internet. It was a fantastic project that had gathered records from just about every public place around the country and put them all in the same database, then cross-referenced it all."

"Wow, that was some work."

"It was," Dan said. "For example, I know what degrees both of you have from university records, what was on your last driver's licenses from an Oregon database, and your last known addresses."

"And you've tapped into this data just to find out about people?" Carey asked.

"Actually, no," Dan said, smiling at her. "But it does come in handy for meeting new survivors like you two. The database was activated and backed up in three different places because it will help in the body recovery and location of graves for the future reference work. That data will be the starting point when we actually begin putting all these poor souls into final resting places. We'll add into the data the information about how we found the person, and where exactly they are buried."

Matt glanced at Carey. She could tell from the look in his eyes that he was impressed. And she was amazed that after just two days how much they could talk to each other simply with a look.

"If we did come to work for you," Matt said, getting the conversation back on track, "what exactly would that entail?"

"You mean hours and such?" Dan asked.

Matt nodded.

"Actually, as many or as few as you wanted to put in. At this point, everyone is sort of in this together. We're going to be helping each other set up places to live, begin food distribution of salvaged items, and so on. To be honest, what we're discovering is that people want to work on this too much, and we end up having to make people slow down, take time off."

"Are you trying to match skills to jobs needed?" Carey asked.

"As much as the skills allow," Dan said, nodding.

One of the men working on connections under a table covered in electronic equipment laughed. "Yeah, I was a plumber in Vegas. I'll be glad when I can get back to pipes. This wiring stuff is for the birds."

Everyone laughed.

"We've got almost twenty thousand people headed here over the next six months," Dan said, "and with luck, even more after that. We need everything in the way of skills, and all the help we can get to give everyone a place to live, clean water, electricity, and enough food."

Carey could feel herself getting excited. Society might not be completely dead after all, if this worked. And even if it didn't, it was worth the fight. She certainly had nothing else to do.

"You know my degrees," she said to Dan.

"I certainly do, Dr. Noack," Dan said.

Carey sat back. She had been a post-doc. Granted, she had a Ph.D., but no one had ever called her doctor before. It took her a few seconds to take that inside.

Matt smiled fondly at her, clearly trying not to laugh at how Dan had surprised her.

"I'm not so sure I like the doctor stuff," she said, ignoring Matt for the moment, "but since you know I have that degree, what could I do to help? I doubt you're going to be doing much work in electromagnetics at any time in the near future."

Dan actually laughed. "You're young, you're smart, and you know computers and how to do research. We're going to be reinventing a lot of wheels over the next ten years, if you know what I mean. We're going to need scientists, people who know how to keep thinking ahead, as well as take information from the past and apply it now."

Then, before she could say anything more, he turned to Matt. "And you, Mr. Landel, are also a real find for us. Not counting your education in electrical engineering, your ability with electronics would help us a great deal. I assume the cameras on the poles near the freeways are part of your security system?"

Now it was Carey's turn to try not to laugh at Matt's shocked look.

"They are," Matt said.

"And keeping a building the size of the Baxter building in water, electricity, and a working elevator, all by yourself, isn't an easy task. Yet you managed that as well. In case you haven't noticed, I'm almost begging you to come and help us."

"Dan," the plumber guy said from under the panel, "I'll join you on my knees if it helps get him on board, so I can go back to my pipes."

Everyone in the room laughed again.

Carey could tell that Matt was shocked they knew so much about him, and how he had been living. It surprised her as well, until she remembered the power of those satellites orbiting overhead. As Matt had said, they probably knew what vegetables he picked for dinner out of his garden.

Dan went on with his pitch. "I'm not saying this isn't going to be a lot of work. It will be. Some of it will be just basic work, like helping deal with the bodies. And for nothing more than you could do for yourself over the first few years, since it will be some time before we have a money system again."

"There is planning for one?" Carey asked, shocked.

Dan nodded. "There is. Everything we do is aiming at a longer term goal of getting back to farming, manufacturing, and all the other infrastructure it takes to supply the needs of all the survivors."

"Is this military?" Carey asked, realizing there were some pretty basic questions they hadn't gotten to yet. "Did the United States Government survive?"

"It did, sort of," Dan said. "No one in congress or the executive branch survived that we know of."

Carey was not surprised at that news. No one on the planet thought the wave of energy coming toward Earth could be dangerous. It had been just another day, with another strange thing happening out in space.

"Right now everything around the country is just being run as you see it here," Dan said, "a sort of volunteer work project, half directed by a military structure because of the nature of the majority of who survived. After each of the five cities are populated again, we'll have local elections, and those governments will take over, with the military side stepping back into a sort of police function. The first national election is slated for five years from two days ago, on the eighth anniversary of the disaster. We'll elect a new President and Congress then, starting over with five states at first."

Matt glanced over at Carey. She knew, without a doubt, she wanted to help Dan and the others. Something like this was so much better than sitting alone on the beach, wondering how she was going to die alone.

But she didn't want to commit unless Matt did. She had decided on her way up the sidewalk that she wanted to be with him more than she wanted to help Dan and the rest.

"Well?" she asked Matt, "what do you think?"

Matt smiled at her, the excitement in his eyes. "I'm in if you are."

Carey turned to face Dan. "I think you just found two more volunteers."

"Wonderful," Dan said, clapping his hands.

From under the electrical equipment came the sound of applause.

"We only have one delay in starting," Matt said, smiling at Carey. "It's going to take us a few days to get Carey and her cats moved over here from the coast."

"Oh, that's right," Carey said, annoyed at herself for forgetting that she actually didn't live here, and that her cats were expecting her to come back soon.

"You've been living on the coast?" Dan asked. "What area?"

"North of Depoe Bay," she said.

"Can you fish?" he asked.

"Well," Carey said, glancing at Matt, then back at Dan. "I've managed to catch my share of crab and dig my share of clams. And I used a Native American net system near the mouth of a small stream for other fish. But beyond that, I wouldn't have a clue."

"Well, I was hoping," Dan said, smiling. "One plan we have is to set up a supply line for fish from the coast sometime over the next six months."

"I don't think I'd be much help in that area," Carey said, remembering her cold mornings trying to get anything out of the ocean to eat that was fresh. More often than not she had come away empty handed.

"Well, take as much time as you need," Dan said. "Just hurry back, we need you."

"I'll get moved as quickly as I can," she said.

"If you need help, just find me," Dan said.

"Actually," Matt said, "if you could lend us two motorcycles, that would be a large help."

Carey managed to not shout *No!* She would have to

climb over her fear of the things and learn how to ride. Until most roads were cleared, it was going to be the main way to travel any real distance.

"Not a problem," Dan said. "I'll have two waiting for you on the sidewalk in front of the Hilton."

"Great, thanks," Matt said. "And no problem with me continuing to live right where I'm at?"

"None that I can think of," Dan said, shrugging. "I don't think we're going to be dealing with a housing shortage anytime soon. Our plans are to spread out in this area, and into the Northwest section, where there is a lot of single-family housing."

"One more thing," Matt said, glancing at Carey. "If I start working for you, I could use a little help with another project I have going."

Dan looked puzzled, but Carey smiled, knowing what Matt was about to say.

"I've been raising some chickens," Matt said.

That stopped all activity in the room almost instantly.

"Fried chicken," one man said.

"Eggs," another said. "I can't remember the last time I ate eggs."

"Well," Matt said, "with a little help on feeding and harvesting the eggs, and some good management, I don't think that's going to be a problem for the future. I have about five hundred or so birds trapped in the Rose Garden. I think that place can hold a lot more than that if I have help with feeding."

Carey could have cut the thick silence that filled the room.

Finally, one man said, "Sorry, Dan, I'm going to work for him. He's got fresh chickens."

Everyone laughed, and Dan smiled even larger. "I

have no doubt we can find more than enough people to help with the chicken project. I'm *very* glad you two are joining us."

"I'm glad you're here and doing all this," Matt said.

"So am I," Carey said. "It's amazing what having a hope for a future can do for the spirit."

"That, and a piece of fried chicken," the man under the desk said.

THIRTY

DAN WALKED THEM to the doorway, shook both their hands, and told them to hurry back. Carey felt as if he actually meant it. Nice to be wanted again.

Then she and Matt were back in the mid-morning heat, headed down the hill. They were a block into the walk before either one of them spoke, but Carey didn't care. She was thinking about what Dan had said, about the promise of a new government, towns with social aspects, people gathering and having families and surviving. Even if only a part of it happened, it was fantastic.

Now all she had to do to get to work helping this cause was to learn how to ride a motorcycle, get her cats, and then find a place to live.

Or maybe in a different order, now that she thought about it. Having a place to go to when she got back here to the city might be a good idea first.

Finally, as they crossed the second street headed down the hill toward the Baxter building, Matt broke the silence.

"Looks like we have jobs again."

"Retirement just isn't the life of luxury it's made out

to be," Carey said. "I just have to figure out where to live."

"I'm assuming you don't want to go back to your old apartment," Matt said.

"No," she said, surprised at how firmly that came out. "Although I wouldn't mind getting some things from there at some point. And from my parent's home as well."

The idea of actually having some of her old possessions again pleased her, and got her a little excited. Everything she had on the coast, besides the cats, could just stay there, to maybe be used later. It could be her coast retreat when she needed to get away. She wanted to start fresh here, with new things combined with old stuff from her past.

"I can help you with finding a place," Matt said, smiling at her. "I have an idea on where you might want to live."

"Where?" she asked, glancing at him. He had this impish look in his eyes she hadn't seen before.

Was he going to suggest that they live together? Or that she take one of his spare bedrooms? It would temp her, she knew that. But it also might be too close, too soon, even with the way she felt about him.

But if he asked, right at this moment, she didn't honestly know what she would say. That's how much she had come to like, maybe even love, this man.

"Let me show it to you first," he said. "I think you might like it. And it has some advantages."

His smile told her that no amount of coaxing was going to get his idea out of him, so she didn't even try.

They made it the last few blocks back to the Baxter building in silence, and when they got on the elevator, her stomach was fluttering. She didn't know what she would say if he asked her to live with him. The idea felt right, and really wrong at the same time.

"Matt," she said, her voice shaking a little, "I don't know if—."

Instead of punching the button for his apartment on the twenty-second floor, he punched the button for the twentieth floor.

"Yes?" he asked, smiling, more than likely knowing exactly what she was going to try to stammer out.

"Nothing," she said, now even more confused.

The elevator opened on a foyer area with two large, double doors on each end. Matt moved toward the doors labeled "A", pushed them open, and walked inside.

"Someone was living in "B" when I moved in," Matt said, walking ahead of her. "I took care of their bodies when I cleared the building. But this place was empty. I could never figure out what to do with it, since I'm using all the space on the two floors above. I think this is almost better than my apartment."

Carey stood in the door and just stared. She had found her home, she knew it without even stepping inside. The apartment had a big kitchen area, floating in the center of a large tiled space like Matt's kitchen. The windows were floor-to-ceiling and over ten feet tall, giving the large living and dining area almost a cavern feel, since it was empty.

The carpet was a light brown, and everything was trimmed in beautiful oak. An oak desk surrounded by massive bookcases covered one interior wall.

Matt walked to the kitchen counter and ran his finger through the layer of dust. "It will take us some time to clean it and wash the carpets, but otherwise it's in good shape."

She moved over and stood beside him, staring at the

fantastic space, the view of Mt. Hood in the sunlight, the river spread out below the apartment, the city basking in the first day of its new future.

"I can get the power hooked up here easily," he said. "The plumbing might take a little more, but I think that if I can't make it work, then that guy fighting the wiring back in the communications room might help."

He turned and took her hand, looking her squarely in the eyes. "I'm being selfish here," he said. "I'm hoping you'll stay close, so we can really get a chance to know each other."

"I want the same thing," she said, squeezing his hand gently, but not letting go. She liked the feel of his skin against hers, and the powerful feel of his hand in hers. "And I'll make you a deal."

He smiled, taking her other hand in his so that they now faced each other. "Always interested in deals."

The closeness of him made her want to get even closer, to pull him against her fully and kiss him. But somehow she managed not to. Instead she kept talking.

"If I move in here, you'll have to let me help you with both of your gardens and the chickens, in exchange for vegetables and meat, of course."

"Another thing I was hoping you would say. We both are going to be working. Keeping up gardens the size I have is going to get to be more work than I want to do alone."

"And I'll do some extra cleaning around the building in exchange for you keeping the water and power flowing. That fair?"

"I think I'm getting the better part of that deal," he said, smiling at her.

"So we have a deal?"

"We have a deal," he said. "I'm just glad you like

this place. I have, from the moment I first walked in here. I've been in every room in the building and my place and this place are the two best by a long ways."

She laughed. "It seems from the moment we met you've been helping me find a place to stay."

"It's been my pleasure," he said, staring into her eyes as he squeezed both of her hands lightly.

"Thank you," she said. "Without your help I might have missed this chance at a new future."

With that, she pulled him toward her, keeping his hands in hers.

She kissed him, letting her body press against his.

She held the kiss longer than she had intended. Actually a lot longer. She just didn't want to let go of the wonderful sensations that were surging through her, the feeling of his lips against hers, the way his body fit against her.

He didn't push, he didn't object, he didn't pull away. Instead, they seemed to become one in that kiss.

After a moment, or maybe hours for all she knew, she ended the kiss and eased back from him, feeling the loss of his lips on hers.

She felt hot, and she had no doubt that her face was flushed. The empty apartment around them suddenly felt very, very warm.

That had been some kiss. Best she had ever had.

Ever.

Matt's face was also flushed, and the surprise in his eyes was wonderful.

They stood there, close, hands grasped, staring into each other's eyes for a long moment, then she decided that she either needed to break this up or she would end up kissing him again.

And again.

She stepped completely back and let go of his hands.

"You know," she said, proud that her voice only broke once as she tired to speak, "we're going to have to do something about the air-conditioning in here as well."

All Matt could do was stand there and nod as she turned to explore the bedrooms and bathrooms of her new home.

THIRTY-ONE

MATT WATCHED CAREY as she worked on building them two salads for lunch. He had added in a couple pieces of cold chicken from last night's dinner and poured them both diet Coke to drink. He was now sitting at the table, waiting and watching her. He couldn't imagine ever getting tired of watching her.

That kiss, thanking him for his help, had left him stunned and almost gasping, just like his first kiss back in junior high had done. Everything about Carey stunned him. Never in his life, not with any past love or infatuation, had he ever felt so strongly for a person. Not only did he want to take her in his arms and make love to her, but he wanted to talk to her over meals, walk with her through the city, work beside her.

He just wanted to be with her.

And that scared him a lot. This wasn't like him, falling so hard after only knowing a woman for a couple of days. He needed to take a deep breath and try to separate out how many of his feelings were from being alone for three years, and how much was truly feelings for Carey, the person, the woman. That separation was going to take a lot longer than two days.

And now, by asking her to move into the apartment on the twentieth floor, he had just risked his entire world here in this building. If she turned out to be some nut case, he was going to have to move out. But he just couldn't imagine, no matter how hard he tried, Carey being anything but what he was seeing.

But that got him right back to not trusting his own emotions, mostly because the emotions that he had used to deal with other people had been shut off for so long.

One thing that encouraged him, more than he wanted to admit, actually, was her worry about getting too close to him too fast. It seemed odd, but he considered her worry a very good sign that she was sane.

She slid his salad in front of him. It looked wonderful. Fresh tomatoes, lettuce, sprouts, and some sliced cucumbers, all topped with an oil dressing, and garnished with sliced hardboiled eggs.

And it had been prepared by someone else. The salad was better looking than anything he would have gotten in most restaurants, back when there were restaurants.

Maybe someday there would be restaurants again. He just hoped when that day came, he would be sitting across the booth from Carey.

"This looks fantastic," he said, grabbing his fork and digging in.

"Thanks," she said. There was a moment of silence and then she went on. "I've got a confession to make."

Her voice was full of worry.

He glanced up. She was playing with her salad, sort of moving lettuce around but not seeming to care if she ate anything.

"Oh, oh," he said, trying to make light of the sinking feeling he had in his stomach. Every time a woman had said that "she had a confession to make" to him in the past, it had meant trouble, and things changing. He was liking the way things were heading at the moment between them. He didn't need any confessions, but it looked as if he was going to get one.

"Go ahead."

She looked up at him, a forkful of salad in her hand. Then as if blurting out the worst crime imaginable, she said, "I don't know how to ride a motorcycle. In fact, I'm afraid of them."

He stared at her for a moment, shocked that that was all she was worried about. Then, even though he knew he shouldn't, he laughed.

"It's not funny," she said, still not putting the forkful of salad in her mouth. "Motorcycles are the only way we're going to get to the coast and back with any speed. The roads are a mess all the way. And I've been thinking about it. We need to take two bikes so that we can get both of my cats back here."

He could see how upset this had her. It was no wonder she had picked coming with him yesterday over being on her own with people on motorcycles coming into town. Beyond her friend getting hurt from the bikers, she had a real phobia about motorcycles that she had clearly never dealt with.

So, what could he do to help her?

"Maybe I should just walk back," Carey said, still clearly upset. "You go to work to help Dan and I'll figure out a way to get the two cats back here to Portland. I could rig up some sort of child's wagon and just pull it with them in it."

"Does that mean you would rather I not help you?" he asked, afraid of the answer.

"Oh, no," she said. "I want you to help me. I just

have this problem with motorcycles, and that's the only logical way we both can go, besides both of us walking. I just don't see how I can learn to drive one of them. At least not quick enough to do us any good on these roads."

"Actually," he said, "we only need one bike. All you have to do is ride behind me."

He reached across the table and put his hand on her arm. He wanted to stroke that soft, light skin, but instead he used his touch to try to calm her.

She shook her head. "We can't get two cat carriers on one motorcycle with both of us on it as well." Then she looked at him with a questioning look. "Can we?"

"Sure we can," he said. "Do you have much else at your place on the coast that you want to bring back, besides the cats?"

"Nothing really," she said, shaking her head. She paused for a long moment, then said, "Maybe a few small things that would fit in my backpack. The rest can be left for some future use. I'll furnish the apartment here with new stuff, and things from my old apartment and parent's home."

"Then it's not a worry," he said. "Problem solved. One of those big bikes is enough. Keeping the cats from totally freaking out on a motorcycle is another matter altogether."

"They will just have to deal with it," Carey said. "If I have to, they have to." She tried to smile at him, but the smile didn't reach her eyes as it normally did.

He took his hand away from her arm and made a show of going back to eating, trying to make her believe that it wasn't a problem. Actually, it wasn't. And he had no doubt that once they had been headed to the coast for a few hours, she would be comfortable on the bike as well, and past her fear. But he now knew he was going to have to take it very easy at the start, and work with her fear to get them going. He could do that.

"Okay," she said, her voice hesitant. "You've ridden motorcycles before?"

"A bunch of times," he said, taking a bite of a chicken leg. "That's why I just assumed you had as well."

"Okay," she said again.

He could tell she didn't like the idea of getting on a motorcycle. And right now he needed to give her an out. "Look, if the motorcycle doesn't work for you, we'll find other ways of getting there and back. You walked here, didn't you? I want to go with you, if you want me along, and walking is no problem as far as I'm concerned. Dan will just have to wait for us. We really aren't in any great rush."

She thought for a moment, then nodded. "I suppose you're right. We're not in that much of a hurry, are we? Dan will put us to work no matter when we show up."

"Of that I have no doubt," Matt said. "Let's just play it by ear and see how the trip goes. If the motorcycle works, fine. If it doesn't, that's fine as well. The focus is getting your cats, and getting all of us back here safely. Right?"

"Right," she said, smiling at him.

"But I would suggest," Matt said, "that we get your new place set up, and at least partially furnished before we leave. That way you and your cats have a place that is comfortable to come back to."

"Good idea," she said. "And the first thing is cleaning."

Matt laughed. "That, and power, and water, and air-conditioning."

"Oh, yeah, those too," she said, shaking her head and smiling. This time the smile reached her eyes.

"There may not be a housing shortage for all the new people coming in, but I bet there's a cleaning and maintenance shortage."

"Now we know why Dan wants us as soon as we're ready," he said. "Cleaning help."

"More than likely," Carey said, taking the last piece of cold chicken off the plate. "And you know, I won't mind in the slightest."

Matt realized he wouldn't either. Cleaning homes and getting a city ready to be reborn seemed a lot more valuable a job than putting in security cameras in bank vaults. Of course, doing that had given him the chance to survive.

And to meet Carey.

THIRTY-TWO

CAREY HAD JUST FINISHED wiping down the three bedrooms and the walk-in closet, and was just about to start on the hallway when the lights came on.

The cleaning had been doing great. She had had to carry three buckets of water from Matt's apartment so far, and she had no doubt she was going to be carrying more before she was finished.

Actually, the fact that the apartment had been completely empty helped a lot. No furniture or old drapes or bedding to have to take care of. Just walls, counters, and windows. She would vacuum last.

She and Matt had replaced light bulbs in all the ceiling fixtures, then he had gone off to see if he could hook this apartment into his electrical system. She had worried that it would overload it, but he had brushed the comment away.

"Trust me," he had said, "those three generators on the roof could handle this entire building if they were forced to."

She would have to trust him, as if she hadn't trusted him enough already.

She wiped the sweat off her face and stood looking

at the room that would be her bedroom. She loved her new place, more now that she was working in it. It just felt good, even empty. And the light from the tall windows in the main room was amazing, almost as if she was outside. She loved places that were filled with light, and now she had found one. Even the master bedroom had huge windows.

She would have never been able to afford an apartment like this one when everyone was alive, let alone furnish this much space. It was only because she had survived, and everything was free that she could do this.

But she had survived, and since there was no one left to protest, she felt she deserved this beautiful place. It would just sit here and go to waste if she didn't use it.

"It seems we have light," Matt said, coming through the double front door. "And come over here and feel this."

He motioned her to follow him. He led her to a vent in the wall beside the pantry door. He showed her where to put her hand.

The cool air coming from the vent sent chills through her hot, sweating body. "Oh, a miracle worker."

"Don't say that until I get the water running," he said, laughing. "Electrical is easy for me. Plumbing, on the other hand, is a nightmare. Luckily I did most of the heavy lifting getting water to the two floors above you. With luck, this floor will be easy to open up as well."

"Just don't flood my new apartment," she said, smiling at him as she sat down on the floor in front of the cool air, letting it blow over her. She hadn't realized just how hot she had gotten washing down the walls and windows.

"No worry there," he said. "But I take no bets on the

basement. Thermostat for temperature is room-by-room. You might want to check them."

"Thanks," she said. "I will. Would you toss me that water bottle? I think I just want to sit here and get chilled."

"You have a thing about heat, don't you?" he said, laughing as he grabbed the water bottle from the kitchen counter and handed it to her.

"I didn't used to," she said. "But three years living on the Oregon coast will do that to you. Trust me, you'll be freezing when we get over there, after this kind of heat here."

"It's not going to be that much difference," he said.

"Now it's your turn to trust me," she said, smiling at him as she finished taking a long drink. "If it's this hot here, more than likely the coast is socked in with a fog, and the temperature is a cold fifty-five to sixty. Of course, that's also the temperature of a winter day when it's below freezing here, but that's beside the point."

"Amazing what a hundred miles can mean to climate," he said, shaking his head.

"A hundred miles and an ocean," she said. "But give me enough time and I'll get used to this climate again."

"I think we have all the time in the world," he said. "Now I'm going to go see if I can figure out a way to turn on your water."

"Thanks," she said. "And good luck."

She watched him walk out the door. He had the build of an athlete, was clearly in very good physical shape, and carried himself well. She remembered the wonderful feel of that body against hers when she had kissed him. She hoped that at some point soon, she would be against him again.

And kissing him again.

She took another long drink of water, letting the cold draft of air brush over her arms and neck and face. Then she stood, feeling the sweat that had dried on her skin crack. She hoped he got her shower running soon, or she was going to have to borrow his again.

She had finished wiping down the walls and was starting on vacuuming the carpets with his vacuum cleaner when Matt came back through the door. He arms were covered in grease, some of which had made it to black streaks across his face.

She flicked off the machine and smiled at him, wiping sweat from her face. "Any luck?"

"Time to test this and find out," he said, heading toward the kitchen sink. He took one of her dirty towels and used it to protect the sink handle from the grease on his hands. He twisted the cold open and then waited, leaning down to listen.

No water came out at first, but by the time she had moved over beside him, the water was flowing through the tap.

At first it was red and dirty in color, but then it quickly changed to a clean look.

Matt nodded. "Get all the taps running, about half open, including the shower and the bathtub and the utility sink, and leave them running. I'm going to go check to see if I have any leaks where I brought the pipes to this floor into my system."

She did as she was told, and by the time she was finished, the apartment sounded like it had a bubbling stream running down the hall. And all the water looked clean, from every tap, almost instantly.

Matt came back in a few minutes later, smiling. "No leaks."

"Water looks great here," she said.

"Good. Let's turn them off."

Together they turned off every faucet, with Matt checking each one to make sure it worked, and that there were no leaks in the drains under the counters.

Then, as they headed back for the kitchen, he said, "I'm going down to a store about six blocks from here, off of Front Street, to get a new water heater."

"The old one won't work?" she asked. She had no idea at all about plumbing.

"I doubt it would after having water sitting in it for three years without movement."

"Oh," she said. "Do you need help?"

"I have my little tractor with the bucket on the front," Matt said, smiling. "And I have a good path cleared through the car wrecks to that store. I'll just load a water heater into the bucket and bring it up the freight elevator. I might need some help getting the thing from the elevator in here."

"Just shout when you get back," she said.

"I will." Then he moved over closer to one of the big windows and pointed across the river. "The next wave of settlers is arriving."

She joined him, staring at the dots that were bikes moving along the freeway toward the bridge. The crews working to clear the road had made it past that point, so the bunch of bikers were moving at a pretty reasonable speed.

Again the sight of them twisted her stomach, even though she knew who they were, and why they were here. She was going to have to get over this fear of motorcycles at some point. It was silly and she knew it. More than likely, on the trip to the coast, she would get past it. At least, she hoped that would be the case.

"Looks like we're at the end of a new Oregon Trail,"

Matt said. "They're not quite in covered wagons, but close."

"Same reason, though," she said. "They are coming here searching for a new home to start over."

"That's true," Matt said. "More than likely, a hundred years from now they'll be writing history books about Dan and those folks out there, and their trek to Oregon."

"I hope so," she said. "I sure hope so."

THIRTY-THREE

IT WAS AMAZING how much plumbing a guy could learn out of books. Matt was actually starting to gain some confidence with it. And considering the only thing he had done with plumbing before three years ago was pour Drano down a sink, he was doing all right. Better than all right if he said so himself. It sometimes took him a few tries before he got a joint to not leak, but this time he'd gotten it right the first time.

Amazing. Simply amazing.

Adding her apartment onto his closed water system turned out to be easier than he had expected. He just opened a few values he had closed off before, and ran a pipe from his clean water system to the main line to her apartment. He installed a shut-off valve as well just in case something happened in the future.

No leaks anywhere. He checked it three times because he couldn't believe it.

Carey helped him move the new water heater into her place and drain the old one. It still weighed a lot and it took both of them to get it into the bucket of his tractor out into the dumpster area behind the building. Doing that, he discovered that Carey was a lot stronger than she appeared. That was a good thing to know, considering the world they were living in.

Then he hooked up the new water heater without a problem, watching for any leaks as the water moved into it.

"You're going to have to give it some time to heat up the water," he said, sounding like he knew what he was doing. He hoped he did. He had read the installation instructions at the hardware store twice.

"Then I'm going to need to borrow your shower again," she said, "if you don't mind. Even with the air-conditioning on, cleaning this place was hot work."

"But it looks great," he said, slowly scanning the apartment. And it did look good. She had even managed to wash the inside of the windows while he was off getting the water heater. The apartment smelled of lemon cleaning solution and was as bright and shiny as if it had just been painted.

"It does, doesn't it?" she said, smiling. "This is a simply wonderful place."

"I thought you'd like it," he said. "I sure do."

"I do more than like it," she said. "I love it. Thanks, for everything."

"You're welcome," he said, smiling at her. She seemed radiant as she studied her new place, the fear she had shown at lunch now gone. "But it needs furniture, don't you think?"

"Not today," she said. "It has to be over ninety degrees out there. If you don't mind, I'd like to take a shower, help cook a nice dinner for the both of us, and maybe watch another movie. We can get some basic furniture and supplies tomorrow morning when it's cool."

"You know," he said, "that sounds like a perfect evening to end a perfect day."

"A perfect day is doing plumbing?" she asked, smiling at him with that twinkle in her eye that he was starting to love.

"No, a perfect day is being with you all day and not having any leaks in the plumbing."

She laughed. "You sure know how to charm a girl. So what do you have up in that wonderful kitchen of yours that I might help cook for dinner?"

"I always have more chicken," he said. "And I make a mean spaghetti sauce from scratch."

He watched her as she thought about the choices, then said, "I seem to remember I used to do a pretty good lemon and herb chicken. How does that, with some asparagus out of your garden done in a light cream sauce, all served with a salad, sound to you?"

He laughed. "No leaks and asparagus in a cream sauce. Now I know I'm having a perfect day."

"Well then," she said, "I'll get the chicken defrosting and then take a shower."

"I'll do one more quick check of the water system and be right behind you."

He didn't offer to wash her back, but he wanted to.

THIRTY-FOUR

EATING DINNER with someone besides her cats felt great, and after just a few meals, it was starting to feel almost normal. She would have never thought that possible three days ago. Dreamed about it, maybe, but never thought it would happen.

Her lemon chicken tasted better than she remembered it tasting, and the asparagus and sauce came out perfectly. She almost felt human again after the shower, and while the chicken cooked and Matt took a shower, she had gone back down to her apartment to just walk slowly through it. She had no doubt, she would be very comfortable here. Actually, more than comfortable. This was a dream apartment for her. She could see herself living here the rest of her life.

When she got back to Matt's, she checked on dinner, then wandered into the security room. A large group, maybe the biggest yet, were coming into town, the motorcycles seeming to stretch into the distance. The sight of them jarred her again, but not as much as the first time she saw the bikes. And this time there was no fear making her want to run away. Knowing who they were helped. And seeing that there were young children and a few babies in this group made them seem very non-threatening.

Humanity rebuilding itself, getting up off the mat from the knockout blow and fighting on.

Matt joined her a minute later, his hair wet and combed back. He looked so damn good, she just wanted to kiss him right there.

Instead, she pointed at his monitors. "More company."

"Wow, that's a lot of people," he said. "Am I glad we went and talked to Dan. Sitting here and seeing this without knowing what was happening would be really scary."

"True," she said. "Now it looks hopeful."

"That it does," Matt said.

At that moment a timer dinged from the kitchen, calling them to dinner.

About halfway through the wonderful dinner, they switched the conversation over to when they should leave for the coast.

"You know," she said, realizing what she had been feeling when she was downstairs while dinner cooked, "the furniture in my place isn't really that important to have in place before we get back. I'd rather take my time and get some stuff I really liked. Cat boxes is all that needs to be ready, if you don't mind me crashing on your couch the day we get back."

Matt smiled. "Not at all. Consider my place as yours until we get you set up."

"Thank you," she said, keeping her gaze locked with his for a moment. "For everything."

"Trust me," he said, smiling that smile that she was growing quickly to love. "It's been my pleasure." He paused for a moment, then said, "Missing your cats, huh?"

"Very much," she said. "And getting worried about them." More worried than she wanted to admit. It felt like she had been gone a lifetime in just the last two days.

"So, we roll out real early tomorrow morning. Buddy's got a spare cat box he hasn't used that I'm sure he wouldn't mind loaning the new neighbors."

She laughed. "What we do for our cats."

Later, she once again fell asleep on his shoulder while watching a movie. But this time, when he tried to cover her with a blanket, she woke up enough to pull him down to her and kiss him again.

Long and hard.

It was a perfect kiss, far, far better than she had ever imagined or dreamed since this nightmare of a world had started.

After a few minutes, he picked her up and carried her into his bedroom, kissing her all the way.

Slowly, very slowly, they undressed each other and all she could do was marvel at how wonderful he was, how perfectly built, how great his skin felt against hers.

And how wonderfully he kissed.

Two hours later, she fell asleep once again, this time nude in his arms.

Somehow the nightmare of the last three years had turned into a wonderful dream.

And for the first time in years, she had no desire to wake up.

THIRTY-FIVE

THE FANTASTIC SMELL of toast and sizzling eggs woke her. The sun wasn't over the mountains to the east yet, and Matt was gone.

She stretched and lay there smiling, remembering how wonderful everything had been with Matt last night. The fear that she was moving too fast now completely gone. That made no sense considering that she had only known him for a few days, but somehow she knew him in far deeper ways than just being together.

They had both survived the last three years and there was a new world lying in front of them to help build. And build together.

She climbed out of bed and wrapped the bathrobe Matt had draped across the bottom of the bed around her, then walked barefoot down the hall into the kitchen.

Matt saw her coming and smiled that wonderful smile that she knew she was never going to tire of seeing.

"I was hoping to serve you breakfast in bed."

"After last night, I'm not sure I could have handled that as well."

He laughed and came over and kissed her, then quickly went back to the eggs, indicating she should take a seat at the table. He had already showered and was dressed.

"Isn't this awfully early?" she asked, noticing that the lights were still on because the sun was a distance from being up.

"I figured we'd get an early start for the coast before it got too hot," he said.

The image of him naked beside her was pushed aside by the sudden realization that very shortly she was going to have to climb on a motorcycle.

He smiled, not really laughing, but clearly almost reading her thoughts. "Don't worry, I'm doing the driving and we'll get your cats back here soon, I promise."

"Thanks," she said as he slid a plate of scrambled eggs and toast in front of her. The smell was wonderful and the plate had barely stopped moving before she had the first bite to her mouth.

The idea of riding a motorcycle just scared her to death, but that seemed just silly now considering what she had already come through. And for the first time she had someone in her life she could trust.

Granted, she really didn't know him yet, not completely, but she felt she did, and she felt she could trust him. And right now that was enough.

More than enough.

Outside, she could see movement on the interstate bridge. Clearly humanity was up and working early as well, getting the highway cleared and working to build a new future.

And she needed to do that as well.

She needed to move into a future because suddenly

she had one again. With Matt and with all the people pouring into town.

She took a deep breath. She had survived three years alone in all the death and destruction. She had come up with the courage to come back to Portland, to meet Matt, and to join the rebuilding.

She could ride a motorcycle and face whatever else needed to be done in the coming years.

Just as she had done coming into town just a few days earlier, she slotted her fears away and felt a calmness come over her.

She finished the last bite of her eggs and pushed the plate aside.

She stood and kissed Matt hard, not allowing him to come up for air for a good thirty seconds.

"Thank you for breakfast."

All he could do was nod and smile.

Then she started toward the bathroom to take a shower. About halfway down the hallway she stopped and looked back at Matt. "I can be showered and dressed and ready to go in about fifteen minutes."

Then she slipped the robe off, holding it in one hand as she stood there naked, smiling at the shocked look on Matt's face. "But I don't think we need to leave for thirty minutes if you'd like to scrub my back."

She turned to the bathroom grinning as behind her Matt scrambled to his feet and followed.

One hour later, she was in the passenger seat of a motorcycle, holding onto the man of her dreams as they headed off into their future.

A future she never dreamed she might have.

Following is a sample chapter from the next book in the Seeders Universe series, *Against Time*.

CALLIE SHERIDAN felt a sense of relief that she could finally see the light ahead. More than she imagined she would feel, considering she had enjoyed the three days down in the Oregon Caves. A real change and a relief from her normal grind of research and teaching undergrad classes in Paleontology at the University of Oregon in Eugene.

But after three days completely in the dark and damp of the cave, she was ready to see some natural light once again, even if it was just a rainy Oregon day.

She and the two graduate students with her had gotten permission from the Forest Service to go into a special area of the Oregon Caves complex, far off the normal tourist trails. It had taken them almost four of hours of hiking just to get to the tiny room. There they had been allowed to dig for signs of fish skeletons preserved in the rocks of the cave.

One of the students, Jim Williams, was in his final

year, working on his thesis, married, with a child in Eugene. He stood no more than five six, shorter than Callie by a couple of inches, and had bright red hair. From the pictures Callie had seen of his new child, the red hair had moved on a generation.

Barb Hillcrest still had over a year in school to get to her thesis. Barb was a solid woman and towered over Callie at over six feet. Barb lived alone with three cats and was worried about getting back to them.

Callie liked them both, and both had turned out to be hard, hard workers during the entire time in the cave. Both had focused their studies in vertebrate paleontology, which was Callie's specialty.

The Oregon Caves had been formed out of granite instead of normal limestone and was a gold mine for fossils from various times in history. It had taken her almost a year to get the permission from the Forest Service for the short surface dig. A cave specialist and park ranger named Dave had gone with them to make sure that they wouldn't disturb anything in the cave with their dig except around one small area tucked in the back of a small cave.

Dave was a middle-aged guy with a gut and gray hair and had a fantastic sense of humor that kept them laughing, even though he must have been bored to tears with their conversations at times and the excitements over finds of tiny fossils.

On the way in he had kept them entertained with his stories of the cave and the names of the different rooms and how they had been named. For a pretty long distance into the cave the path had been covered with asphalt and was an easy walk, with some stair climbing and one bridge over a stream called The River Styx.

Now they were all carrying out some great samples

in their backpacks that would keep them busy for months at school. The trip was a great success and she honestly had no idea what they might have found.

Dave had decided that instead of having them climb out the tourist exit where the tours left, he'd have them just backtrack to the way they had come in. As they neared the front entrance to the cave, Dave suddenly shouted "Karen!" and ran forward.

He had been leading the group up the incline on the asphalt trail that wound through some rock fall, so Callie couldn't see what he had seen.

The light from the small cave opening was bright, even though it had an airlock on it. So someone must have left the door open.

Callie shielded her eyes, carefully watching her step as she went forward to make sure she stayed on the asphalt.

Suddenly both Barb and Jim ran up behind Dave, who was now kneeling over a woman who looked to be Dave's age. She also wore a park ranger uniform like Dave's. Her gray hair had been cut short and she looked like she had been beautiful in her day.

But now she was sprawled on the ground in the middle of the asphalt trail and to Callie she looked very dead.

And smelled dead as well.

Behind Karen, scattered along the trail were a dozen more people, all sprawled in various positions and all very dead. Clearly this Karen had been leading a walking tour into the cave with a bunch of tourists when something really awful happened.

Callie quickly checked out a couple of other bodies, an older couple wearing heavy coats. There were no obvious marks on them and no blood.

Callie stepped back and just stood, staring at the bodies, trying to make sense of what she was seeing.

He stomach was twisted into a knot and she wanted to just get sick. Never had she seen so much death in one place. Seeing something like this on television was something, standing here staring at the dead bodies and smelling the rot starting to take over was another matter completely.

Was this some sort of elaborate practical joke?

She looked around the rocks scattered through the cave mouth, but saw nothing that looked out of place.

Could someone have been this sick to do this sort of joke?

She moved back a few more steps closer to her two students and Dave where he now held Karen in his lap and was sobbing.

Callie had been around dead animals and a couple dead humans in her time, and this smell was very, very real and going to get worse, much worse, very soon. These people had been laying here dead for at least a day, maybe slightly longer.

How was that even possible, in the middle of a tourist attraction during a busy season?

As Callie looked along the group of dead, eleven men, women and one teenage boy, she could tell a few animals had worked at ones closest to the cave entrance, since it was braced open by the body of a man laying face down on the asphalt.

More than anything she wanted to be sick. This was not a pretty sight. But she had to stay clear in her thoughts for the moment. There would be time for re-acting later.

She just couldn't imagine what might have caused

this and why no one had come for these people and bodies.

This made no sense at all.

None.

She covered her nose with her sleeve and tried to think.

Then suddenly one very ugly word popped into her head.

Gas.

"We need to get out of here now!" she shouted to her students and Dave. "Move past the bodies quickly, don't look at them. Get up the trail to the parking lot."

"What do you think caused this?" Barb asked, clearly stunned, but moving.

"Might be gas," Callie said. "Jim, help me with Dave."

They both went to pull Dave away from the body of a woman named Karen, but he brushed them aside, angry.

"No, I'm staying with her."

"Dave," Callie said, "there's nothing you can do for her."

"I don't care," he said, looking up at Callie, his eyes full of tears. "She's my wife. I'm staying."

"We'll send help," Jim said.

Callie nodded, but doubted that they would find help as quickly as Jim made it sound. Something here was very, very wrong.

Callie motioned for Jim to follow Barb up the trail and past the bodies.

Without a look back at the man holding his very dead wife or at the bodies she passed, Callie followed her two graduate students up and into the light.

Outside the big trees looked normal, the day was beautiful, a slight breeze blowing among the pine.

It felt normal.

And that scared Callie even more.

All three of them took off running up the paved path through the trees, following the signs that said "Parking Lot."

It took them only a minute at full run for the three of them to reach the wide, paved parking lot.

Callie expected police and everything else to be there, but instead the lot felt deserted.

Two bodies lay sprawled near one car.

Around them the towering mountains stretched upwards, leaving most of the parking lot tucked into the side of the hill in shadow.

Callie made herself stop, take a deep breath to clear her mind, and then look around for anything that seemed wrong or out of place.

Nothing.

A beautiful afternoon in the Oregon Mountains.

Except for the two bodies sprawled in the parking lot.

"What happened?" Barb asked, her voice shaking.

It was clear Barb was barely holding it together. But Callie had no answers for her. All Callie could do was stand there on the edge of the parking lot, staring at the bodies and shaking her head.

She had no idea what had happened.

But she had no doubt now that this was a lot bigger than some poison gas in the mouth of a cave.

A lot bigger.

NEWSLETTER SIGN-UP

Be the first to know!

Just sign up for the Dean Wesley Smith newsletter, and keep up with the latest news, releases and so much more —even the occasional giveaway.

So, what are you waiting for? To sign up go to deanwesleysmith.com.

But wait! There's more. Sign up for the WMG Publishing newsletter, too, and get the latest news and releases from all of the WMG authors and lines, including Kristine Kathryn Rusch, Kristine Grayson, Kris Nelscott, *Fiction River: An Original Anthology Magazine, Smith's Monthly, Pulphouse Fiction Magazine,* and so much more.

To sign up go to wmgpublishing.com.

ABOUT THE AUTHOR

Considered one of the most prolific writers working in modern fiction, *USA Today* bestselling writer Dean Wesley Smith published almost two hundred novels in forty years, and hundreds and hundreds of short stories across many genres.

At the moment he produces novels in several major series, including the time travel Thunder Mountain novels set in the Old West, the galaxy-spanning Seeders Universe series, the urban fantasy Ghost of a Chance series, a superhero series starring Poker Boy, and a mystery series featuring the retired detectives of the Cold Poker Gang.

His monthly magazine, *Smith's Monthly*, which consists of only his own fiction, premiered in October 2013 and offers readers more than 70,000 words per issue, including a new and original novel every month.

During his career, Dean also wrote a couple dozen *Star Trek* novels, the only two original *Men in Black* novels, Spider-Man and X-Men novels, plus novels set in gaming and television worlds. Writing with his wife Kristine Kathryn Rusch under the name Kathryn Wesley, he wrote the novel for the NBC miniseries The Tenth Kingdom and other books for *Hallmark Hall of Fame* movies.

He wrote novels under dozens of pen names in the worlds of comic books and movies, including novelizations of almost a dozen films, from *The Final Fantasy* to *Steel* to *Rundown*.

Dean also worked as a fiction editor off and on, starting at Pulphouse Publishing, then at *VB Tech Journal*, then Pocket Books, and now at WMG Publishing, where he and Kristine Kathryn Rusch serve as series editors for the acclaimed *Fiction River* anthology series, which launched in 2013. In 2018, WMG Publishing Inc. launched the first issue of the reincarnated *Pulphouse Fiction Magazine,* with Dean reprising his role as editor.

For more information about Dean's books and ongoing projects, please visit his website at www. deanwesleysmith.com and sign up for his newsletter.

www.ingramcontent.com/pod-product-compliance
Lightning Source LLC
Chambersburg PA
CBHW011934130726
47904CB00014B/2487